WHITE FLAG OF THE DEAD BOOK V

DEAD SURGE

JOSEPH TALLUTO

PROLOGUE

As the sun finally dipped below the horizon, Dutch Smallwood stepped out of his farmhouse. The day had been warm, and the cool evening air felt good on his sweaty skin. The growing corn was coming in well, better than it had in years. The other crops he had going were doing pretty well, too. Over the last few winters, his wife had become fairly skilled at canning, so food for the family had never become a problem. Meat was still on the scarce side, but it showed up on the supper table more often than not. All in all, things were relatively normal, except for the dead getting up and walking around.

Dutch and his family had survived the Upheaval in good shape, as did most of his neighbors. The isolation of the typical American farm didn't give the virus which created the ravenous corpses much of a toehold. The farm folk figured out what was happening, and in their independent, self-reliant manner, did what they needed to do to survive.

Dutch realized he'd never be able to use all of the acreage of his fifteen hundred acre farm, so he took his tractor and dug a six foot ditch around his farmhouse and fifty acres. He left the rest of the land to grow wild, giving cover to numerous small game animals and providing a source of meat for his family.

His neighbors followed suit, and they helped each other out as much as possible. Dutch had been with his friend Carl when they checked on a nearby farm. That family had turned. Dutch figured the son, who had returned home from college, had brought the disease with him. Dutch was forced to kill his neighbors and burn down the house.

After that, Smallwood and his family hunkered down and decided to wait it out. They had food, water from the well, and electricity from the windmill and generator. That was six years ago.

Dutch thought about those things as he walked his ditch line. The path was worn smooth from countless hours of sentry duty, but Dutch did it every night anyway. He shouldered his pick and moved into the darkening shadows of the evening. Experience had taught him that the dead had a hard time seeing in the dusk, and since there was no breeze, his scent wouldn't carry, either. Occasionally, he would find a ghoul in his ditch, clawing uselessly at the steep sides, unable to climb out. Dutch would snap a quick hit with his pick, and retrieve the corpse later for burning.

He rounded the corner and heard a ruckus in the henhouse. He hadn't seen a coyote for years, so Dutch made a mental note to check on the silly birds when he got back to the yard. In the gloom, he never saw the wide swath of flattened grass which came out of the ditch and stretched towards the farm.

Dutch turned the last corner and started for home. By now, the darkness was deep and the only light was from a hurricane lamp they used in the kitchen. The soft yellow glow spilled out over the back porch and backyard, gently lighting the henhouse.

Reminded of the cluckers, Dutch moved that way, past his garage and workshop. The livestock barn loomed large in the back of the farm, and the grain bins looked white in the rising moonlight. The cornstalks clicked softly in the wind.

Dutch stopped by the henhouse. The once noisy birds were now silent, and when he looked down, he understood why. All of his chickens had been slaughtered, their carcasses torn apart and scattered in the feed yard. Fresh blood glistened in the moonlight, soaking into the dry earth, blackening the dirt.

Smallwood looked around quickly, trying to see if the coyote was still near. The corn clicked again and Dutch looked up, seeing small movements in the stalks. With a sickening feeling, he suddenly realized there wasn't any wind. Something was in the corn, making it move.

Dutch threw away his pick and spun for the house. His rifle was there and he was suddenly very afraid.

He took two steps and something slammed into his back, knocking him forward and off his feet. As he landed on the ground, a small part of his brain realized that whatever hit him had jumped from the roof of the henhouse. Whatever had killed his birds was now on top of him!

Dutch struggled to turn over when he felt a searing pain in the back of his neck. Warm blood flowed down his back and neck when another pain ripped through him from a second bite.

In desperation, Dutch swung his arm wildly behind him, knocking off his attacker and allowing him to get to his knees. He twisted around in time for something to slam into him again. This time it locked its teeth into his throat. Blood loss from his two other wounds caused him to be weak and unable to resist. He raised his arms feebly, but could not pull off his attacker. Blackness began covering his vision as he fell back, his attacker still on top of him. The last thing he saw were a pair of glowing eyes.

Dutch never heard his family die screaming from the sudden attack.

CHAPTER 1

"Push. Push! Okay, now step back, don't get your legs tangled up."

"Like this?"

"Perfect. Bring your hands back to the ready position."

"Where's that?"

"Not again. C'mon, Jake. Right hand by your side, left hand forward on your staff."

"Like this?"

"Better. Now bring up the spike end, good. Strike!"

Jake brought the staff up over his head and jammed the metal spike down towards his imaginary foe. I had decided when he was about five years old to start training him on how to defend himself against an attack by the undead. I knew he wasn't strong enough to kill a zombie at the time, but he could generate enough leverage to trip one and get away.

As he grew older and stronger, I had shifted his training to killing a downed Z. We trained a few times a week, working on making his motions more reflex than conscious thought, but being seven years old, it took a few times for the lessons to sink in.

On the other side of the patio wall, I could hear Charlie work with his daughter Julia. We had tried working the kids together, but they ended up trying to hit each other with the sticks, so we separated. Julia was a year younger than Jake was, but she took to the training as if she was born to it. Charlie began wondering aloud if she might be ready to take on a zombie, but his wife Rebecca heard him once and that was the end of that.

Jake wiped the sweat off his head and looked sideways at me with his big brown eyes. He reminded me of his birth mother when he did that, and made it hard to refuse the question I knew was coming.

"When can I kill a real zombie?"

I looked around for Sarah, his stepmother. When I saw the coast was clear, I whispered "Soon. When you're ready."

Jake's shoulders slumped slightly, and he looked away towards the patio wall, where a clacking sound could be heard. Charlie sparred with Julia as part of her training, and I figured it was time for Jake to spar as well.

"Put the staff away and then come on back," I said, taking off my pistol and placing on the nearby table.

"Are we fighting?" Jake asked, suddenly eager.

"We'd better, or Julia will kick your butt again."

Jake scowled. "She cheated!" But he ran to put his staff on the rack by the door.

When he returned, we began sparring, Jake throwing punches and kicks, and me blocking and instructing. I taught him holds and how to break holds, and we practiced those as well. One thing Jake was really good at was kicking. His balance was excellent, and he could kick several times without putting his foot down. That was a fooler sometimes, because after a kick, you expected a reprieve, not another kick.

"John or Charlie?" The radio called from the table.

I raised a hand to stop Jake's next attack and picked up the radio. "Go ahead, Tommy."

"Duncan says he thinks he may have spotted a Z down by the river."

"Whereabouts?"

"West side of the driveway, about fifty yards out."

I thought about that for a second, getting my mental bearings. "Okay, we'll take a look. How are the repairs coming?" One of the cows got spooked and rammed into the fence on the island that served as our primary pasture and rendezvous point.

"Almost there. Stupid cow busted three fence posts." Tommy sounded properly disgusted.

"Understood. John out." I put the walkie away just in time to see Charlie walking around the corner with Julia. Even though she was his adopted daughter, she actually looked enough like him to be confused as his real daughter.

"Everything alright? I heard the radio," Charlie said, tousling Jake's hair. Jake ducked under the hand, grabbed his staff, and squared off against Julia, who grinned in anticipation and brought up her own staff.

"Tommy says Duncan may have spotted a Z down by the west side of the driveway," I said, putting my holster back on. "I'll take a look and see what's up."

Charlie nodded. "I'll come with you. Brush is kind of thick on that end."

I gladly accepted the help. Charlie was one of the best woodsman I had ever met, and if he wanted to take a walk in the woods with me, all to the good.

"Are you going to fight a zombie?" Jake asked, as we turned and headed them to the lodge.

"I'm just going to see if there is someone down there who shouldn't be, that's all," I said, looking over at Charlie who didn't help by grinning at me. Before the words left my mouth, I knew what was coming next.

"Can I come with? Please?" Jake turned and walked backwards, turning on the full power of his brown eyes.

Julia, while being a year younger, quickly understood what was going on and added her voice to the proceedings. "Can I go, too? Please, Dad? Please? I promise I'll stay out of the way and I won't tell Mom."

I looked over at Charlie who was trying to figure out what to say and stated, "Why not? Probably your Uncle Duncan chasing shadows again." About a year ago, Duncan was convinced there was a zombie along the river. He spent three days in the mud before he finally admitted defeat.

Before we reached the house, I gave some instructions to the youngsters. "We are going to get our gear. You two stay here and practice quietly until we come and get you. If you get out of hand, you can't go. Understood?"

The two little warriors stood at attention and tried to salute me. Charlie bit his hand trying not to laugh, and I had a hell of a time suppressing a giggle at the kids.

"Good. Wait here." Charlie and I went into the lodge and over to our supply room. I grabbed my ever-present pack and my melee weapon, a well-used garden pickax. I belted on my new knife, having broken my old one, stupidly trying to lever open a door. The new knife had a curving blade of thirteen inches, and was more of a short sword than a knife, but it killed just as well. I grabbed an extra box of ammo out of habit, and moved to the patio. I didn't bother with a carbine, figuring it to be either a loner or nothing at all. Charlie left his long gun behind as well.

The kids immediately stopped sparring on our appearance, and we headed as a group down the big stairway that led from the lodge to the floor of the river valley. Starved Rock was a beautiful collection of cliffs, caves, waterfalls and rock falls, and had been our home for six years. Originally a state park, it was now our permanent home. If a better place existed for remote living, I hadn't seen it.

At the bottom of the stairs, Charlie and I spread out a little, each of us trailing a youngster. Jake and Julia were literally bouncing with excitement. They had been born to the Upheaval, and they were growing up in the aftermath of the Zombie War. They had never known a world without the undead. Jake had been with me from the beginning, and he knew no fear of the zombies. To him, they were just part of his life and needed to be dealt with.

In a way, I envied him. He never gave any thought to what a zombie might have been before they turned, never gave a whit about whom they might know or what they might have seen. He just saw them as something to be removed. To be sure, he knew how dangerous they were and he wasn't about to try and pet one, but he didn't get that deep feeling of dread and fear when the ghouls were lurking about.

CHAPTER 2

We crossed the parking lot and worked our way down the driveway. According to Tommy, Duncan thought he saw the intruder on the other side of the road that led to Utica.

As we walked, Jake was peppering me with seven-year-old questions.

"Do you think it will be a big zombie?"

"Don't know if it's a zombie, Jake."

"What about a little zombie, those fast ones?"

"Don't know if it's a zombie, Jake."

"If there's more than one, can I kill it?"

"Don't know if it's a zombie, Jake, and no, you can't."

"What if there's five or six?"

"Then your Uncle Charlie and I will have a lot of work to do." I turned around and faced Jake. "Listen buddy, I know you're excited, but you have to control it, because a zombie can hear you a long way away."

"Like those?" Jake pointed over my shoulder.

I stood up and spun around, bringing my pick to bear. Sure enough, three zombies came stumbling out of the woods, two of them crashing to earth when they tried to cross the ditch by the roadside. Charlie hustled Julia over to Jake, and then unsheathed his tomahawks. As he started for the Z's, I faced the two kids. Their faces were calm, but I could see white knuckles as they gripped their staffs.

"Stay here, and don't yell or do anything. We'll be back in a second. Keep your sticks at the ready." I advised as I turned to the fight. Charlie was finishing off the second ditch jumper as I approached and aimed for the third. I was about to protest his greedy nature when two more zombies burst out of the trees on right, directly in front of me. I barely had time to land a backhanded swing on the head of the first one, when the second got close enough to grab the handle of my pick.

I pushed on the handle, but not before the zombie, a grim grey specimen of indeterminate gender, managed to moan in my face. Habit forced me to exhale quickly and turn my head, trying to minimize the exposure to any virus-laden spittle or other fluids I didn't want to think about.

I let go of the handle as I pushed, and quickly drew my knife. As I stepped forward, I saw Charlie finish off the third on one his side. I waited a half second for the zombie to turn over to gain his feet, and when his neck was exposed, I stabbed downward, severing his spine. He collapsed onto the pavement with a smack, and I stabbed again into his skull, finishing him.

I looked over at Charlie and he nodded at me. But his smile turned to a look of alarm. It must have been the look on my face, because behind him four more zombies were emerging from the woods.

As I discovered, his look was due to the trio of additional zombies that came out of the woods on my side.

"Son of a bitch!"

"Where the hell did these guys come from?" I asked rhetorically. For all we knew, they had been roaming the river for years, finally coming out and up to our area, attracted by the noise.

"I have no..."

"Dad! Help!"

"Daddy!"

Charlie and I both spun around and our worst nightmare was unfolding before our eyes. Three more zombies had come up from behind, and they were on the verge of surrounding our children. Jake was wide-eyed with fight, and Julia was stepping back from a teenage-looking zombie that snapped its teeth at her.

Jake stuck the end of his staff in the throat of the nearest Z, and pushed with his whole body. The zombie, a taller man in a torn and filthy suit, grasped at empty air as he fell to the ground. The third ghoul was closing in on the side and Jake wasn't going to be able to stop him.

Julia cracked the zombie nearest her on the side of the head, but the Z barely slowed down.

Charlie and I left our battles and ran as hard as we could, both of us drawing our guns at the same time.

"Jake! Julia! Down now!" I yelled. God bless those two, they dropped as if they had been hit with tranquilizers. The zombies took a second to recover from having their dinner drop out of sight, so I fired wildly as I closed the distance, bullets smacking hard into the zombies and knocking them away from the children. Charlie fired as well, and the bullets, while not immediately fatal to all the zombies, had been enough to put them out of the way while we reached the kids.

I grabbed Jake and Charlie grabbed Julia, and we skirted around the writhing Z's on the ground. I checked Jake for any damage while Charlie checked Julia. We ignored the crawling zombies while we tended to our children.

"You okay? Any bites or zombie goo on you?" I asked turning the boy around.

"I'm fine, didja see me push the zombie?" Jake asked.

I let out a long breath of relief. "Okay, I need you to take Julia back to the house. Let me have your staff."

Jake looked at me with big brown eyes. "But it's mine! I didn't do anything wrong!"

I glanced at the advancing horde and switched magazines in my gun. I had about two minutes before things got interesting. I looked back at Jake. "No, buddy, I did. I need your staff because my stick is over there." I pointed to a prone figure still clutching my pickaxe.

"Oh! Okay! Will I get it back?" Jake still held onto the staff, but not as tightly. Out of the corner of my eye, I could see Charlie giving instructions to Julia, who was nodding dutifully.

"You bet. Now I want you and Julia to run to the guesthouse and stay there. Don't stop and don't look back, understand?"

"Okay! C'mon Julia"! Jake took Julia by the hand and Charlie and I watched for a second to make sure nothing else came out of the woods at them. When they were halfway to the guesthouse, formerly the Visitor Center of Starved Rock, we turned our attention to the advancing dead.

CHAPTER 3

"Close one," Charlie instructed, holding a tomahawk in each hand.

"Too close. You gonna tell Rebecca?"

"As much as you're going to tell Sarah."

"Agreed. Let's get to work." I spun the staff and jammed the steel cap though the skull of the nearest zombie. It had been hit in the spine, paralyzing its legs, but it still tried to crawl towards us. Charlie finished off the one that had been advancing on Julia, and the third had been hit with a lucky shot in the head, putting her down for good.

The rest of the zombies had made good time, and were actually spreading out to try and prevent our escape. It never worked, since they couldn't move as quickly as we could, but I had to give them props for trying.

We didn't use our guns as much as we used to, saving them for emergencies or desperate situations, but with a small band like this, we'd stick to hand-to-hand. We'd been fighting zombies for six years, with the last three being nothing but daily fights. We'd seen some strange things, but this was nothing spectacular.

"I'll start on the left," Charlie said. As soon as he said that, he exploded into action. He darted around to the far left of the line and ducked low, cracking his 'hawk into the back of the knee of the first zombie. It tumbled down and he hit it with the second 'hawk before it even hit the ground.

I turned my attention to my side and attacked the furthest right zombie. It was a woman, maybe, but since they all were turning a deep shade of grey it was hard to tell. The newer ones still looked like people, just bloodier. If they wearing distinct clothing, it was easier and much easier if they were naked, but that was actually rare. I rammed the point of the staff into the eye of the Z, bursting the eye socket and piercing the brain. I pulled it out as it fell and levered the staff between the legs of the next one. A quick turn tumbled that one down, and I let the staff go, since the third was getting way too close. I whipped out my knife and stabbed the zombie in the neck, figuring to punch the spinal cord and drop the smelly bastard.

Good theory, but didn't work in practice. I must have missed, because the Z just kept coming with my knife sticking out of its neck. Its hands grabbed my left arm and pulled me in for an infected bite. I grabbed the left wrist of the zombie and twisted it inward, forcing the Z's elbow towards its face and away from mine. I used my right hand to grab the handle of my knife and pulled it out as I levered the zombie to the ground. That wasn't easy with it still grabbing my forearm. But I gained enough space to jam the blade into the top of the zombie's skull and shut him down.

I stepped back quickly, just managing to avoid a grab on my leg by the zombie I had knocked down earlier. I brought my foot up and slammed it down on the neck of the Z, pinning it to the pavement. A quick stab finished it off and I looked for the next foe.

Charlie had done well on his side, killing two of his zombies and removing the third. The fourth, an older gent in his Bermuda shorts and black socks, shuffled towards Charlie with an outsized groan.

I stepped up behind the zombie, and just as Charlie stood up and cocked his arm back for a killing blow with his 'hawk, I swung my knife in a wide, backhanded sweep that completely removed the head of the zombie. It stumbled back over its butt and bounced on the ground, with the rest falling towards Charlie. The head still bit and snarled, but I finished it off with a jab to the temple. My new knife was well suited for both slashing and stabbing.

"Nice one." Charlie admired. "I need to get a new knife. I like the way that one cuts."

"Talk to Duncan. He seems to know more than anyone about knives and blades," I said, retrieving Jake's staff. If I left it behind, I'd never hear the end of it.

"Come on; let's drag them over to the pit."

"Haven't used that place in a while," Charlie said grabbing two Z's by the collar and pulling them along the driveway.

I joined him with two of my own. "That's for sure. Wonder where they came from?"

"Could be anywhere. Fall is nearly here, so they could have been in the woods all summer, or been following the river from a bigger, dead town." Charlie dumped the bodies in and started walking back for more.

"Maybe. Just weird to see so many in a group around here. Hope it's not a sign something bigger is happening," I said, looking to the West.

Charlie read my thoughts. "I'm sure the gates are holding on the passes. Nothing will get through the mountains."

"Hope so." I thought about it as I grabbed two more zombies for the pit. "It would suck to have to do that all over again."

"No thanks," Said Charlie. "Once was enough. If I never see Denver again, it will be too soon."

I laughed. "Good God! I nearly forgot about that fight! Thank Heaven for mannequins."

We hauled the rest of the zombies over to the pit and squirted some kerosene on the pile from a squeeze bottle we left hanging in a tree for that purpose. I tossed in a match and as the flames burned brightly, I sanitized the end of Jake's staff and my pickaxe. My knife I would clean back at the lodge. Charlie would do the same with his 'hawks.

We walked back to the Visitor Center and collected our young. Jake wanted to hold his staff, because Julia had hers, but relented when I refused in a voice that brooked no argument.

As we entered the clearing on our way to the stairs, I looked up and saw Sarah and Rebecca standing on the first landing of the stairs. Both of them had rifles in their hands, and they were holding them at the low ready.

I waved up to the ladies, followed by Charlie, but didn't get one in return. Instead, Sarah and Rebecca turned on their heels and walked back to the lodge. There was tautness to their movements that did not bode well for Charlie and myself.

Oh, well. I'd been in trouble before and will be again. That seemed to be the nature of things, although Sarah was lately more impatient with me. I wasn't sure why it was, but I was sure it had something to do with the communication we had received from the capital.

CHAPTER 4

Charlie and I hustled the kids into the lodge ahead of us, and we stopped at a small maintenance shed for the ritualistic burning of our weapons. I lay out my knife, pick, and Jake's staff, and sprayed kerosene on the parts that had killed zombies. Charlie did the same with his tomahawks. I struck a match and touched each weapon, watching as the flames burned bright red, and then settled to a normal white-orange. I blew out the flames once the red died out. I always sanitized Jake's stuff twice, just to be sure. The virus, we learned, burned crimson, so it was easy to tell when it was gone.

Once the weapons had been cleansed, I took a piece of steel wool and buffed off the scorch marks. I inspected my knife for nicks, and then slid it home in its sheath. The sheath rode along my waistline and required a draw out from my back as opposed to across my body, but it all worked out the same.

We went into the main hall of the lodge and Sarah was sitting at the big table. Jake and Julia were playing in the corner, building a small universe out of plastic blocks. Janna and her daughter were over by the fireplace, waiting for Duncan to come home, and Angela was nearby with her and Tommy's son. Rebecca was sitting by Sarah and neither looked happy. Charlie and I passed the table, and took off our gear in the supply room. For some reason I was suddenly tired, and not in any mood for nonsense regarding the safety of my son.

I went back to the table and sat down, not saying anything for a while, just reorganizing my thoughts.

Sarah didn't give me much time. "We heard shots. What happened?" Her green eyes were angry, and I couldn't blame her entirely, but it wasn't the best approach.

"We got the call that there might have been a lurker along the river. I went to take a look and Charlie came along. Since we thought it was only one, we figured the kids could come with. We got ambushed by a good sized group," I said simply, shifting my back to a more comfortable position.

Sarah looked concerned. "Ambushed? How many? Where?" If she was angry before it was gone now. From her perch on the stairs, she couldn't have seen the fight.

"There were fifteen of them, and before you ask, I have no idea where they came from." I was on edge myself, which was normal after a fight these days, and the implications of a large zombie group in my backyard didn't present any positive news.

"How did Jake get there?" Sarah asked, shifting the conversation.

I had anticipated this and answered quickly. "He and Julia came along when Charlie and I thought it was only a single Z. If it had been reported that there was that many, do you honestly think I would have brought either of them?"

Sarah looked at me for a minute, and then must have decided against further argument. Her tone softened. "You're right. You going to tell me about it?"

I thought a minute about how close the two kids had come to being bitten, and decided to skip half the truth. "Same thing we've seen before. We were among them before they moved, and we sent the kids back to the Visitor Center when it became obvious it was a serious fight."

"Well, I'm glad you're all okay," Rebecca said, ending the matter. All I could hope for was Jake to keep quiet until he forgot about it, and then we'd be in the clear.

"Do we want to talk about the communication from the capital?" Sarah asked, turning the attention back on me.

I stood up and went over to the message board, which was nothing more than a legal pad. I brought it back and laid it on the table, three heads craned to see what I had written there when the message first came in. NEED TO TALK TO PRES, PROB IN THE PLAINS, COMMS DOWN, NO REPLIES. I had long had a habit of scripting when I spoke on a phone, a 'cover my butt' move from my days as an administrator. With phone service very limited, and still being sorted out by people who didn't know what they were doing yet, the fact that we had a call at all was pretty amazing. Most people these days used CB radios, ham radios, and walkie-talkies. Communities that had power were able to activate their phone networks, but it was an iffy thing. Rumor was there was a phone service survivor somewhere in the southern states, but he was busy.

After reading the message, the three other heads at the table turned to look at me and I shrugged my shoulders. "I guess the polite thing to do would be go see what the president wants," I said.

Sarah looked at me. "When are you going?"

I leveled a look back at her. "We're going so you can hear for yourself." As she arched an eyebrow at me, I tilted my head at Charlie. "Coming along?"

Charlie looked at Rebecca and back to me. He nodded and winked at Rebecca, who brightened at the thought of a trip.

I wasn't fooling anyone. Sarah knew I had invited her and Rebecca along as a barricade to any unreasonable requests. God knows I'd had a few of those. When I accepted the position of President four years ago, I knew it was going to be rough. But the last three years had been unbelievable, with the Zombie War. We had been to nearly every major part of the United States, and fought hundreds of zombie battles. I constantly told myself I would write down a chronology of the War, but so far hadn't got around to it. While it wouldn't be a best seller, at least it would be a lesson to those who come after us on what worked, what didn't work, and how not to get yourself killed when three hundred zombies come after you.

We went to bed and in the morning prepared the boat for travel. The highways were mostly cleared, and people travelled well on them, but there were occasional snags, especially around formerly well-populated areas. But I personally liked using the waterways, and it provided a more direct route to the capital.

Jake and Julia were sad not to be going, but they were happy to be having a special day with their Uncle Mike and their cousins Logan and Annie, over at the other lodge. Mike had moved his family over there and it worked out pretty well. Logan was ten years old, and was becoming quite the little woodsman. He was constantly out in the reserve, checking things out, finding out how things worked. Annie was more of a homebody, helping with the other little ones, my other son included. Aaron was mine and Sarah's son, born on the road and raised with the sound of zombie fighting in his ears. He was tall for his age, with dark hair and green eyes. While Jake rushed in, Aaron was the watcher, waiting for his opportunity. I was curious to see how he took to training, but I had a suspicion he would do well. He was a quiet, deliberate boy, more given to playing by himself than with others, although they liked him and wanted to include him. He just seemed to prefer his own company.

CHAPTER 5

Tommy, Duncan, and Mike came down to the dock to see us off. We were packed light, although thanks to the recent dance we were armed heavily. I was packing my .45, having finally surrendered my SIG to the Zombie Wars. Sarah was armed with a .45 as well, although hers was a Commander size. When she showed a preference for it, I reminded her of the .22 that she used to carry and how far she had come since then. She reminded me that she could shoot it just as well, thank you very much.

Charlie and Rebecca were both armed, and Charlie and myself additionally carried our rifles. It wasn't far to Leport, but as we had discovered, what we thought was safe sometimes bit us.

Once under way, we relaxed a bit in the cool autumn air. The river still carried traces of its morning mist, and the vegetation was heavy along the banks. We threw waves to the people we saw in the towns along the river, and answered a question or three from early fishermen. Further in, we passed the ruins of Joslin, a town I had ordered destroyed early in my presidency. That place was a constant source of roaming zombies, and we closed it down once and for all. The zombies were still there, but they couldn't get out. The only thing we salvaged was the power plant along the river, and a small crew kept it running at a minimum. It supplied power to several small communities, and would do so until the coal piles ran out, which at current use would happen in three hundred years.

Several boats passed us on our way north, some laden with supplies and trade goods. One was a flatboat, delivering ordered goods from the general warehouse. I waved to the pilot, and he sent back a warm welcome.

Towards the afternoon, we stopped at a small, out of the way place to relieve the call of nature. I wasn't one to just let fly over the gunwales, so we pulled up outside the old Illinois Waterway buildings and tied up to the small dock outside the administration buildings. The buildings covered half the canal, and were in decent shape, but no one was available to run the locks anymore, and they wouldn't serve a purpose if we did.

We all got out and stretched out legs, and Sarah and Rebecca walked off to the far side of the building and went inside. One of the weird things about the Upheaval is the toilets worked pretty much most of the time. If you poured a bucket of water into the tanks, they worked. The world had gone to shit, but you could still flush it down. Go figure.

Charlie and I stepped over to the lock and took turns peeing off the gate. It was a kid thing to do, but what the hell. We turned back to the building when the front door blew open and Rebecca stumbled out, falling to the ground. Sarah was right behind her and tripped over her prone form, tumbling close to the water.

A nasty-looking zombie came bouncing off the closing door. He used to be a teenager, judging by what clothing he had left on him, and the gold chain still dangling around his grey neck. His face was shredded, but his eyes were still functioning. He rammed into the door, pushing it outward, allowing him to exit the building. Behind him, another zombie hit the door; this one was skeletal with an arm cut off at the elbow. The door hadn't closed completely, allowing the second zombie to start coming out.

Rebecca and Sarah recovered from their falls, and squared off against their attackers. Charlie and I stayed back a ways, but had our rifles up and trained on the Z's should the fight look go badly.

"Bet you a gun cleaning Rebecca finishes hers off first," Charlie said out of the side of his mouth.

"Done. Even though she was closer." I had a lot of confidence in Sarah.

Rebecca swung her melee weapon, a three-foot piece of hickory, topped with a ball peen hammer, ground to a point. The metal cracked into the zombie's knee, breaking the joint and tumbling the ghoul to the ground.

Sarah jumped and side-kicked the second zombie in the sternum, propelling him backwards into the building. The zombie slammed backwards and fell down.

Immediately, both Zs struggled to get up, the one without the arm having a bit more difficulty. Sarah stepped forward and used her knife, a seven-inch wonder that could easily remove a hand if needed. The needle tip slid neatly through the eye, puncturing the brain and killing the zombie for good.

Rebecca swung high just as Sarah had stepped forward, and smacked the ghoul right on top of the head. There was a loud crack, and the zombie dropped to the ground, finally at rest.

I looked over at Charlie and we both said the same thing, "Tie." We stepped quickly over to the women and I scanned the interior of the building while Charlie checked the shore for activity.

I turned to Sarah. "All good? What happened?"

Sarah wiped off her blade and sheathed it. "Went to the bathroom and these two came bumbling out. Couldn't tell how many for sure with the echoes in there, so we retreated."

Rebecca spoke up. "If we had been sure there was only two, we'd have stayed and killed them."

No doubt. Sarah and Rebecca were combat veterans of the Zombie Wars and were more than capable of handling themselves. They trained almost as much as Charlie and I did. I looked over the building and saw there was nothing really out of place. These two must have come here infected at some point, and revived inside. Just our bad luck or more to the point, theirs, that we were the first ones to come back to them.

"All right then," I said, turning back towards the boat.

"Wait!" Both women said at the same time.

"What?"

"We still need to use the bathroom." The two women stepped over the zombies and went back inside, finally answering the call of nature.

I looked over at Charlie who just shook his head at me. Fair enough.

CHAPTER 6

We got back in the boat a few minutes later and headed upriver again. I spent a minute thinking about the last couple of days and I couldn't shake the feeling we were in for a wild ride.

Sarah, ever mindful of my moods, sat down next to me and handed me a bottle of water. "Where's your head?" she asked.

I shrugged. "Hoping it's nothing. But I can't shake the feeling we've been handed a warning."

"How so?"

"Well, look at it. We haven't had a zombie inside our perimeter in years, and just yesterday, there were fifteen of the suckers practically on our doorstep. And here today, where you and Rebecca found zombies that in all likelihood shouldn't have been there, and it adds up to some serious portents of things to come." I learned a long time ago to just open up with Sarah. It saved a lot of time.

Sarah's green eyes drifted to the riverside for a minute as she contemplated what I had told her. After a minute, she turned back. "I wish I could tell you it's nothing, John, but this time you may have something." She leaned over and kissed my cheek. "We'll be careful. We've survived the worst this virus had to throw at us. We'll survive this."

I pulled her close as the sun began its quick descent to the horizon. In a couple hours, we would be in darkness and I wanted to get to Leport before then. For all the times I wished my feelings on something were wrong, this time, I really hoped my feelings were wrong.

But I just couldn't shake the notion this one was going to be a doozy, whatever it was.

We pulled into the dock at the southern end of Leport and worked our way up to the first small barricade. A small four-foot fence ran along the riverside, disappearing off into the bend by the overpass. On top of the road were two tall towers, and even in this distance, I could see they were still manned. The sentries up there would warn of any activity within sight, and men would be dispatched to deal with the threat.

The first well-wishers came down to the docks, and I met several people again. One boy in the back ran off in the general direction of the town, and I knew our presence would be reported immediately. However, for now we greeted some old friends, shook hands with a few who had joined us on the long trip west, and more importantly, made it back.

"John Talon!" A voice called out from above. "John Talon!"

I looked up to the hills and saw a small figure waving down at me. I smiled, waved back, and flagged the rest of the crew over. Together, we went up a rather steep incline, passed some lively shops, and made our way to the small Victorian home nestled in the riverside homes that covered the Northern Hills of Leport.

On a wide porch, a middle-aged woman with deep red hair looked at me. She gave me a big grin, and then gave Charlie hug, followed by Rebecca, then Sarah. When she reached me, she took my hand formally, and then gave a slight bow. I returned the favor, and said as I bowed, "Madame President."

Dot's grin widened into a huge smile and she wrapped me up in a big hug. Dot had been elected to the fledgling Presidency after I had declined a second term. Dot was a natural leader, and had an easy way with adults, kids, and dogs. The funny part was she always seemed surprised when people addressed her as 'Madame President.'

"How are you doing, John?" Dot asked, taking me by the elbow and leading me inside. She beckoned everyone else to follow, and inside I saw a table had been set for six people. Dot always knew before anyone else what was going on.

"So far so good," I said, moving to a chair and holding one out for Sarah. Charlie did the same and Dot nodded her silent approval. I couldn't explain it any more than I understood it, but part of me always wanted to have Dot approve of me. I guess it just had something to do with the way I was raised.

"Family okay? I haven't seen your babies in months." Dot sat down and immediately the kitchen door opened. I tensed for a second before I realized it was a couple of teenagers, recruited to work as aides to the President. I remembered my own aides, a couple of young men who followed me out into the battlefield.

We buried one in Omaha, and the other went out to work his own ranch in Arizona.

"Jake's full of beans, and Aaron is getting bigger all the time," I said, looking over the menu. Dot had simple tastes, and the food was hot, filling, and delicious. I knew she had cooked it herself, which made it even better.

"Aaron's a special boy, John. Keep an eye on him, and he'll do great things," Dot said, filling her plate.

I looked over at Sarah, and then filled my own plate, saying nothing. I knew better than to try and get any more out of Dot at that point. Things would work out as they should, and that was the way of it for Dot.

Dot made small talk throughout the dinner, chatting up Charlie and Rebecca. She seemed perfectly suited for her role, and I think the country would move forward pretty well with Dot at the helm. Of course, it was a lot easier to make decisions with only 45 Representatives and 12 Senators.

After dinner, we retired to a side room which had large maps placed up on the walls. I had put them here early on in my administration, marking places which were safe for travel, unsafe for living people, and everything in between. Down the west side of the map, just at the edge of the Rocky Mountains was a large red line. That was as far as we had gone in our war on the zombies. The mountain passes had been closed and nothing undead made it out. On the other side of the country, a similar line had been drawn. This one closed the east coast. However, this one was on the other side of the mountains. And as I looked, it was smaller than I had left it. I guess Dot had been busy in her first year.

On the far wall, another map had been placed over the original. This one was a large representation of the states just west of the Mississippi. Dozens of pins dotted the landscape, and they were all red except for six of them, which were black. They designated six small towns in the far western section of the state of Iowa, just a little south of Omaha. The biggest of the towns I could see was Red Oak. The black dots were nearly a straight line from the west to the east. I had a creepy feeling I knew what they meant.

CHAPTER 7

Dot saw me looking and came over to the map. "Six weeks ago, we lost contact with these towns. On the surface, it didn't seem like much. We chalked it up to bad communication lines. But they happened one after the other, in succession like you see. What do you think?"

I looked at the map again. "Based on what I have here, I'd say you had a new spreading contagion or a group looking to establish themselves in the Breadbasket of America."

"That's what our assessment was, too," Dot said. "We figured it had to be something that was interfering with communication. And these days, the only thing that could do that was lack of people to communicate with."

"So what was causing the problem? I assume you sent someone out there to check." I asked.

"We did."

"So?" I didn't like the way she said that.

"So they didn't come back. Everyone we sent out that way has not communicated with us in weeks, and we're not sure why."

Captured or dead. I thought. "Who did you send?" I asked instead.

Dot sighed. "Jane Coswell, Brian Hernandez, and Bill Osbourne. Each one went with ten people."

I was stunned. I knew all three of them and they were solid, steady people. None of them was likely to screw up a fight or walk into an ambush. I looked back at the map. What the hell was out there?

"Thirty-three people gone." I mused. I looked over at Charlie and I could see he was as shocked as I was. "What do you want from us?" I asked pointedly. I knew what the answer was and I could see Dot knew that I knew. Nevertheless, I wanted to hear the request, just so I could tell myself I had the right of refusal.

Dot looked at me square in the face. "I need to know what's going on, John. I need a crew that can look at a situation and know it for what it is. I need someone to let me know if I have to mobilize the army or send in a crack crew to stage a rescue."

Dot looked away. "I know you've done your part for the country, and no one is more grateful than I." She looked back at me. "I need the best, John, and you and Charlie are it."

I didn't say a word. I stared hard at Dot and she matched me unblinkingly. I knew I was going to lose this fight, but big chunk of me didn't want any part of it.

Finally, I said, "Christ, you don't make it easy, do you Dot?" I looked over at the rest of my companions. "This one's not on me. We need to talk."

Dot nodded and left the room, leaving the four of us to stare at the maps and the pins and what mysteries they represented.

I started the ball. "All right. We've heard the pitch and we know what is expected of us. The question we have on the table is whether or not we take up the challenge."

Charlie looked over the maps then back to me before he spoke. "Something is seriously wrong out there. We know that area, and we know the people that were out there. We know the people that went out there and stayed to settle. None of them could have just been blown over, and none of them would have just up and given up without a fight." He ran a hand over his knife hilt. "Doesn't make sense."

Rebecca spoke next. "We don't know what happened, or what's happening. For all we know, whatever is out there is headed this way and we don't have any way of stopping it." She walked over to Charlie and held his hand. "I guess my fear is not going out, and then wishing we had when we had the chance to take on whatever it is when it was just starting out."

I didn't say anything, but Rebecca had just voiced what I was thinking. While it was easy to say this wasn't my fight, if it was something that stood a chance of wiping out everything I had fought six years for, how could I stand back and just let it go?"

Sarah made the point clearer. "No one says there has to be a fight; all anyone is asking is for someone to take a close look and then high tail it back." Sarah stood in front of me. "I know what you're thinking John, and I understand. Whether we like it or, we have to take this one."

I nodded slowly. "We just figure out what's going on, and then we bug out. Agreed? We let the ones whose job it is now to fight and take care of it."

The rest agreed and we called Dot back in. It took a minute to fill her in on the decision, and I could see she was happy about it. For a second I thought she might have been worried I would say no, but I was probably wrong.

When we took our leave, Dot asked me to stay behind for a second. I told Sarah and the rest I would catch up with them in a minute. We watched them walk further up the hill for a second before Dot spoke.

"Thank you, John."

"You're welcome." I hesitated, and Dot caught it right away.

"Say your piece, John Talon," Dot said kindly.

I gripped the porch rail tightly. "Got a bad feeling about this one, Dot. Got a feeling this one is gonna make the rest of the shit I've been through seem like a vacation."

Dot looked out over the river for a long moment before she spoke.

"Me, too."

CHAPTER 8

The next morning we drew some supplies from the armory and stocked up on some traveling gear. We would take two of our own vehicles, and the decision was going to have to be made as to who was going and who was staying.

All the way back to Starved Rock we talked about the trip and speculated about what might be happening. Charlie was convinced a rogue group was trying to establish themselves in an area before making a play for the big time. Rebecca and Sarah were thinking some kind of crossover contamination was how the animals were getting the virus and we were looking at zombie dogs, cats, or something. I personally didn't want to think that was happening. We had no chance at all as a species, if animals became infected.

I stuck to the notion that it had to be a fresh outbreak that was spreading. It was the only thing that fit the facts as I saw them. The only flaw in my thinking was the loss of thirty-three seasoned fighters. If they were gone, and if my view was correct, the contagion had gotten huge, and we were going to need a hell of a lot of help.

In the end, right before we pulled into the dock, we decided that we needed to be ready for two possibilities: a live one and a dead one.

It was near dusk when we returned to the lodge, and I had to admit I was tired. Tommy and Duncan had a lot of questions, but I had to wave them off until tomorrow. It wasn't fair, and I knew it, but some things needed a night to clear out of your head. I hoped in the morning I wouldn't be as spooked and my bad feeling would be less.

Right before I went to my room, I checked on the boys. Aaron was in a small ball at the foot of the bottom bunk, and Jake was sprawled across the top bunk, snoring softly. I touched each boy once on the head and left the room.

Even with Sarah next to me, sleep was a long time coming, and restless when it did.

In the morning, after everyone had eaten breakfast, I called a meeting for those of us at the lodge. Charlie sat on one side of me, while Sarah took the other. If I didn't know better, I would have sworn Charlie was sticking close in a subconscious effort not to be left behind. He hadn't come on our trip to DC, and we both kind of regretted that decision.

Tommy, Angela, Duncan, and Janna all sat around the table. I didn't include my brother Mike in the discussion. Since he had moved to the other lodge, he had pretty much gone his own way. I didn't mind in the least, everyone makes their own choices. He wouldn't stop being my brother, no matter what happened. In the center of the table, I had spread out a map of Iowa. On the west side of the state, I had circled a large area.

I didn't waste any time. "Here's what we know. Something or someone is causing some problems on the west side of the state. About six towns we know of so far have been lost, overrun, or captured. Three teams of eleven have been sent to this area, never to be heard from again." At this, Tommy and Duncan's eyes got wide. I continued. "Speculation at this point is a new contagion or a rogue group. Dot wants us to go take a look."

"No offense to anyone." Tommy started, "but why us? Why not send in the army, such as it is."

I answered pretty much as Dot had. "A massive group could get the captives killed, and would take too many resources to keep in the field. A smaller reconnaissance group would stand a better chance of staying supplied and moving unseen."

Duncan piped up. "If it isn't a rogue group, and I don't think it is, then a contagion seems more likely. But here's the problem with that. Wouldn't a large contagion attract attention from someone, and get reported?"

I hadn't thought of that, and it made sense. If a large outbreak had happened, someone would have had the presence of mind to flee and report it to the nearest town which would have some form of communication. If it was a contagion, then it was something new, something that wiped out populations very quickly. A new thought occurred to me.

"What if it's airborne now?" I asked quietly. That was our worst fear. A virus contained within bodily fluids can be protected against, but an airborne one was nearly impossible to escape.

Everyone went dead silent as the implications of this possibility sunk in. In this part of the world, the winds typically brought the weather from the west to the east. Looking at the map, the contagion, if that's what it was, was spreading from west to east, so it made a horrific kind of sense.

Charlie spoke first. "I don't think so. We've had heard of it by now, for the same reasons Duncan mentioned. Someone would have figured it out and reported it. Last I knew, there were medical teams out and about, and they would have said something."

I had to agree with Charlie, and was glad to do so. Disease, both old and new, was a constant threat, and now people were spread so far apart. As president, I had implemented a plan to have roving teams of medically trained personnel tour the country in big RVs, servicing communities, delivering babies, and reviving the tradition of house calls. If someone needed major surgery, they were brought into the capital, which had the only surgery center in the area.

"Okay, then we've eliminated the likelihood of a major new contagion. Then what do we have out there?" Sarah asked. "It has to be something that can take out the communications of a town, and be able to silence three teams of hard-core zombie killers."

We all looked at the map and wondered the same thing. What the hell was out there?

Tommy spoke up last. "Since we are looking at possibilities, here's one to consider. We've looked at this from the virus point of view and the living point of view. What about the zombie point of view? We've seen them get a little more intelligent since the Upheaval, with some being able to open doors and others being able to execute a kind of ambush. What if they've evolved further? What if they have become just a little bit smarter? Old style defenses are now useless, because they can just outthink them. That closed door is no longer an obstacle, and that ladder can help them now.

"Jesus," I said, thinking about what that might mean. It would change the nature of how we attack them and adding caution to our side while increasing the deadliness of theirs.

"But it begs the question again. Wouldn't someone have reported it?" Sarah asked.

Rebecca took the question. "Not necessarily. There's a lot of isolated farms in the area, and the communities are fairly spread out as well." She looked at the map. "It would have been nice to know when these towns had lost communication."

"Why?" Charlie asked.

"Because if it was a live group, then there would be a short amount of time between towns losing communication. A walking group of zombies would have taken longer."

Duncan shook his head. "What's next? Are they going to start shooting back, too?"

We all chuckled a bit, grateful for the release of the tension that had been building up.

"All right. So we can figure on preparing for a live problem, that's not too bad. And we have to figure on a dead one, but just something with a new twist," I said. "So the next question is how many and who will be going out on this one. I will be honest. I am nervous, simply because of who and how many have already been lost looking for answers to this little mystery.

"So we have to figure out who's going? Right now, I can say for certain that Janna isn't going because of the baby, Angela for the same reason." Out of the corner of my eye, I saw Sarah begin to stiffen, but I had an answer for that.

"My brother is willing to take everyone over at his lodge, and I think the kids will enjoy the fact that he can turn on the water park now and they can play all day by themselves." The lodge my brother lived in had an indoor water park, and for the last year, he had been working on it, cleaning it out and getting things back in working order. I think his idea was to have a place for people to visit when things eventually returned to normal.

Everyone nodded at that, and it would be a nice change from the routine the kids had grown accustomed to. "So," I continued, "I'm going, Charlie is coming along, Sarah and Rebecca as well." I looked over at Tommy and Duncan. "I'm not speaking for you guys, this one is up to you."

Tommy looked at Angela and she gave him a slight nod. "Count me in. Would hate to see the last few years wasted."

Duncan spoke up. "Same here. Spent too much time out there to see it get wiped out again."

I slapped the table. "Good! Settled then. I have no idea what we're going to encounter, so let's load heavy. We'll be taking the truck and the van. I want to get on the road first thing in the morning."

The group dispersed to gather clothing and supplies, and Sarah hung back to talk with me.

"Thank you for not making me stay behind." She started.

I pulled the maps together. "I have no idea what we're going up against, and I need every solid person I can bring with. Hell, after Denver, you can come with any damn time you please."

Sarah smiled at my compliment. "Who's going to break it to Jake and Aaron?"

I gave her a lopsided grin. "I figured I'd bring them over to the water park this afternoon, let them play a bit, then ask if they want to stay with their Uncle Mike for a week or two."

Sarah thought for a second. "Very clever. They'll never want to leave."

"I have my moments. Few and far in between, but they're there."

"Yes they are."

CHAPTER 9

We spent the rest of the morning and most of the afternoon getting things together and packing the truck and van. Since we had figured to trade or buy much of our foodstuffs, we didn't bring much of that with us. A lot of our gear was ammo and fighting supplies.

Mike was really good about taking the kids and wives. He had more than enough room over there, and the kids couldn't get enough of the water park. Jake and Julia could swim, along with Logan and Annie, and there was a small pool for Aaron to splash around in with the younger kids. I could sense Mike had a longing to go with us, to play a bigger part, but I assured him his part was huge.

"Mike, you have to realize that if something is headed this way, you're going to be busier than hell getting defenses ready. As it is, I need you to think about how we can defend against the worst kind of zombies or renegades."

"Is that what you're going up against?" Mike wanted to know.

"I seriously wish I knew. But we're just going to take a look, then get back here to prepare for it. Dot says the problem is for the army to deal with and I can say I'm fine with that." I was, too. I'd done my bit for king and country, and had only taken this mission because I was doing a favor for an old friend. I hated to admit it, but I was getting older and my luck was only going to hold out for so long. I wanted to see my sons grow up, and running off every day to fight zombies didn't make that future any closer.

Everyone settled in early that night, and sleep was hard to come by. Eventually I drifted off, with my last conscious thought being What the hell is out there? If my dreams were an indication, I should stay home.

In the morning, we dropped the kids off and drove north, looking to take the highway as far as we could. One of the things I put in place as president was the clearing of the major highways. Up to certain points, the roads had been cleared of abandoned and infected cars. We didn't do anything special.

We just pushed them to the side of the road and tipped them on their sides. It had the effect of creating a barrier and in the northern states, a snowdrift fence. There were crews still out there clearing roads. That was their job, and they did it well. Crews rotated in and out to keep things from going crazy, and all of us had taken a turn at road clearing. For reasons too numerous to list, Duncan was no longer allowed near heavy machinery unsupervised.

Across the river was the small town of Utica, and we had cleared it of zombies years ago. However, the town was uninhabited, as a lot of towns were, and it was slowly starting to fade. Trees and grass grew where ordinarily they would have been removed, and a broken window allowed the weather to work on the inside of a building. A couple of homes had collapsed roofs, and several detached garages had been blown over. At some point, we would probably have to fire the town, but it didn't bother us enough yet to work on destroying it.

A quick ride up the hills and we turned onto the highway. The on-ramp was a little tricky, since there were some cracks in the concrete from the effects of winter, but once we got onto I-80 it was smooth going.

CHAPTER 10

Once upon a time, this interstate was crowded with cars and ghouls, people fleeing from destruction only to have it waiting for them down the road. The lucky few who lived away from the major cities managed to do just fine by staying put and hunkering down. The smaller towns out of the way but along the corridor of the interstates got hit with the virus when people carrying it got off the highway looking for refuge.

Out in the far fields, we could see some farms returning to life. Several of the people who had fled the country to the relative safety of the communities were returning to the land, much as their ancestors did after a war.

The vehicles were nothing to attract attention, and nothing that would sustain a zombie assault. Once we figured out they were more of a false sense of security than anything else; we had moved away from those types of things. I was driving the pickup truck that held our supplies and spare gasoline. Charlie was driving the van behind me, and he had the rest of the supplies and the spare ammo.

One of the lessons of the Upheaval was never to put all of your supplies in one place. Too often, people found themselves away from their gear and wound up dehydrating or starving because the zombies surrounded them away from their weapons.

We drove for a couple of hours, and it was nice to see a few other cars and trucks on the road as well. Gas was still in short supply, but it was getting better once we discovered an oil rig still manned in the Gulf of Mexico. After that, it was a lot of research to get the refinery running, and even more research to figure out how to distribute the gas.

With gas relatively scarce, other modes of travel had been explored. Lots of people rode bikes, some returned to the horse, and others just walked. Travel that took hours once now was calculated in days.

We decided to stop in a small town off the main highway. I had no idea what the town was, since the sign announcing it had been hit by something and was just a couple of metal poles in the ground. The town was a one of the thousands that had been hit by the plague. The buildings were weather-beaten and in many cases, broken and falling apart. Old signs of struggles were easily seen if you knew what you were looking for. Over there was a stain on a protected part of a wall. Over here was a small pile of brass casings. The odd bone here and there told the story pretty well, too.

I stopped the truck and got out for a stretch. The van pulled up alongside and the rest of the crew spilled out. Tommy took a quick look around and announced his verdict.

"Well, this one won't be standing long," he said with a grimace.

"Oh, I don't know, a couple of throw pillows, maybe some paint...spruce it right up." Duncan quipped, earning an eye roll from Tommy.

I ignored the two and looked around. The town seemed to be centered around a single intersection. I could see three fast-food places, two car dealerships, and four gas stations. Further up the road was a family restaurant and a decent sized hotel. Like a lot of towns, this one likely sprung up when the highway passed through, connecting rural America with the rest of the world. Who knew that connection, which birthed the town, would one day kill it?

I looked over at Sarah, who was stretching her back out. She caught my eye and mouthed a word at me. I could take a hint.

"Anyone else for bathroom?" I asked.

Rebecca raised her hand, and together the two ladies strolled over to the tall grass on the other side of the vehicles.

"I'm going to take a stroll down the street, anyone want to come along?" I announced to the rest of the guys.

"I'll go," Charlie said. "May as well see what might be seen in this place."

Duncan looked around and snorted. "Good luck. We'll stay here and make sure no one steals our stuff."

We all chuckled at that and moved apart. Charlie and I walked down the center of the street, quietly stepping around bits of debris here and there. Even though our walk was casual, we were constantly searching shadows and corners, looking for any activity.

As the Zombie Wars progressed, we began to see new patterns in the zombie behavior. They started to avoid the outdoors and hang around inside buildings more. Many times, we would go into a seemingly abandoned area, only to find ourselves quickly surrounded. A few nasty surprises like that and a man got quick with his shooting.

At the intersection, there was a single car over on the north side. Its doors were wide open, and a raccoon family looked to have moved into the back seats. Mold was all over the place, and I was sorely tempted to set the thing on fire.

However, a small sign which read "Army/Navy Store" distracted me. Pointing it out to Charlie, we followed the arrow to a small grey building on a single plot near the strip mall. The windows had been smashed open, telling the tale of looting, but it wouldn't be a bad notion to check it out anyway. We had found some really good supply caches in many of these stores, so we hoped this could be another one.

A quick look inside didn't show any zombie activity, and not even Charlie's thrown marble yielded any results. I took point and went inside.

The place was a mess, clothing and patches and pins covered the floor, while the shelves were bare of anything useful. I did find a knife behind the counter and a half box of .45 ammo, but there was nothing else of any relative value. Charlie went a little deeper, checking out the walls and the floor, looking for any anomalies which would signal a possible hiding place.

A door was in the back, which I figured went to a bathroom, but that theory went bust, when I opened another door and that one was a bathroom.

"Got a maybe, Charlie." I called out softly.

Within three seconds, Charlie was next to me.

"Locked?"

I checked the door. "Nope, it's open."

Charlie clicked his teeth. "Might mean someone beat us to it." He mused.

I shrugged. "Might not. Never can tell."

"True. Give her a yank." Charlie pulled his weapon and trained it on the door.

I opened the door quickly and stepped aside, pulling out my pistol at the same time. When Charlie didn't fire right away, I peeked around the door and looked down a flight of stairs.

"I hate dark basements." Charlie sighed.

I didn't blame him. "Shouldn't be too bad," I said. 'I can see light coming into the basement through the windows."

There wasn't much light, but it was enough to see the stairs, and little else. Once we reached the bottom, our eyes would have adjusted enough to be able to see. The only thing I didn't like was the open stairs. It made it very easy to get an ankle grabbed from behind. Once a zombie got hold of your foot, they tended to try and pull the rest of you through the stairs. That tended to upset folks a bit.

I started down the stairs, and behind me, Charlie holstered his gun. He started tapping on the doorframe, trying to stimulate any zombies that might be dormant in the basement.

CHAPTER 11

I'm not sure what was supposed to happen, but suddenly a scream sounded from the darkness, and a shot zipped past my head, burying itself in the ceiling! I ducked back, firing at the spot where I saw the flash. A meaty smack told me I had connected, but how much damage I had done I had no way of knowing. Charlie had yanked his gun out and dropped to the ground, pointing his gun at the darkness, his eyes searching the black for any movement.

"Jesus, what the fuck was that?" I asked as I scrambled around to the other side of the door, keeping my gun trained on the dark.

"Not sure, but I think you hit it." Charlie said, "Listen."

I strained my hearing, and sure enough, I could hear wet, labored breathing. A strained cough reached us and I figured I must have done some serious damage.

"I'll go first," I said, crawling forward and moving at a crouch down the stairs. I moved quickly, trying to keep a low profile and to keep myself from being grabbed. All those stories you scared yourself with when you were a kid suddenly came to life and the covers sure weren't going to protect you now.

I reached the bottom and scanned quickly around. I could see numerous shelves of goods stored down here, so we had a good chance of finding some extra supplies. In the corner, were a pack and a small blanket, obviously where someone had made their bed.

That same someone was breathing their last on the floor in front of me. I knelt down and pushed the gun he had fired at me away. He was crouched in a fetal position, bleeding from a nasty exit wound in his back. A forty-five was unforgiving when it came to wounds.

I knew I couldn't do anything for him, but I tried to get some information from him.

"Who are you? Why did you shoot at me?" I asked.

The man turned his head slowly, blood dribbling out of his mouth. His eyes were vacant, haunted even.

"The teeth.....teeth....click...clicking...." The man breathed a final rattling gasp and his body relaxed slowly in death.

I stood up, and waited for Charlie to join me. He looked at the spreading blood, and said, "Damn."

"Yeah," I said, "Doesn't feel the same, killing a living person."

"Not supposed to," Charlie said quietly. "Wonder why he shot at you? It's not like we came to rob him or anything."

"Don't know. Remember the scream? It was like he was afraid of something."

"Did he say anything before he died?"

I nodded. "Something about teeth and clicking."

"What the hell does that mean?"

"No clue."

"Pity we can't ask him."

"Look, I feel bad enough about this already, okay?" I was getting a little testy. I'll admit I'm a particular kind of gent, one who tends to shoot back when shot at. It's a quirk, for sure, but I'm working on it.

Before Charlie could reply, Tommy's voice came down the stairs.

"You guys all right? We heard the shots." He called.

Charlie answered him. "We're fine. John shot a living guy." Charlie winked at me as I threw him the finger.

"What'd you do that for?" Tommy asked as he came down the stairs. "Damn!" He said as he saw the dead guy.

"Charlie is leaving out the part where he shot at me first. I'm sure his heart would be broken had the man actually managed to shoot me in the head." I replied.

Tommy knelt by the body. "Well, can't blame you for that." He looked closely at the dead man. "Hey, I know this guy!" He exclaimed suddenly.

"You do?" Charlie and I managed to ask at the same time.

"Sure. His name was Pete Desmond. He came with us on the river campaign in the south," Tommy said.

"Solid guy? Prone to panic, at all?" I asked, looking back down.

Tommy snorted. "Not at all. Dude was steady as a rock."

Stranger and stranger. "You don't know what he might have been doing hiding out here?" I wondered.

Tommy shook his head. "He stayed with the military, last I knew. Chances are he was with one of the groups sent out this way by Dot. Too bad we can't ask him."

"Too bad his aim wasn't better. Then you could have," I said, heading back to the stairs.

"Easy," said Charlie.

"Hell with that. Let's bring Duncan down here for a really smartass comment." I left the basement before anyone could reply.

CHAPTER 12

Outside the building, I stood on the sidewalk and looked out over the town. The wind had picked up, and I could see the long grass swaying in the wind. Across the sky, clouds competed with each other to block the sun, and spotted sunshine decorated the landscape. I took a few deep breaths, letting out the tension that had been building. Across the road, I could see Duncan sifting through a hardware store, picking up the odd tool, looking over the scattered leftovers from the first panic of the Upheaval.

Down the street, Rebecca and Sarah were chatting by the vehicles. Sarah saw me and threw me a wave, and I replied with a small wave of my own. I turned my back to her and looked back over the town.

Behind me, I heard someone walking over debris, and a duffle bag was dropped at my feet.

"You all right?" Charlie asked.

I took a deep breath. "Yeah, I'll be fine. Just don't like it, that's all. I mean, not only did I kill a living person, but I killed someone who had managed to survive the Upheaval and the Zombie Wars, and someone who might have been able to tell us what's waiting for us in Iowa."

Charlie blinked. "Well, when you put it that way..."

Tommy came out at that moment carrying a small box. "Hate to break up the therapy, but you might want to take a look at this."

"What is it?" I wondered what Tommy had found.

"The guy downstairs was running scared. He probably thought we were something else." Tommy opened the box and placed it on the ground.

We squatted around the box, and sifted through the meager contents. There was a small canteen, a map, half a box of ammunition, and a knife. That was it.

"I don't get it. What is this stuff?" Charlie asked.

I was wondering the same thing. "Where did you find it?"

Tommy looked at both of us. "This was in his pack. Nothing else."

"Not to sound obvious, but so what? We've travelled light before," Charlie said.

I shook my head. "Not this light. Remember, this wasn't somebody on the run six years ago. This is somebody who would know better. "I stood up and looked to the West. "Something scared the survival instincts right out of this guy."

Tommy and Charlie stood up and we were all silent for a moment.

Finally, Tommy broke the silence. "Well, we do know two things for sure, now."

"What's that?"

"This isn't a rogue group. No way could anyone get scared insane like this guy was. He'd have come out shooting, sure, but not jabbering about...what did you say he said?"

"He said something about teeth and clicking," I said.

Tommy cocked his head to the side. "What do you think that means?"

I shrugged. "It means we still don't know what the hell is waiting for us, or what might be coming right at us."

Charlie pulled out the ammo from the box and put it in his pack. "No point in keeping it waiting. We should go."

I agreed. There was nothing here, especially answers.

Back at the truck, Sarah looked me over and asked what was wrong.

I put away my pack and reloaded my pistol magazine before answering. "Not much, just found some supplies, shot a living guy who might have had answers to our dilemma, and discovered there's something out there that is scaring stupid even veteran survivors," I said, somewhat sharply.

To her credit, Sarah just blinked and said nothing. She knew me well enough to know when I needed to settle this one out myself.

Charlie came to my defense. "Just to clear things up, John nearly took one in the head before he fired back. We all would have done the same."

Sarah nodded. "Let's get going. We should make the Iowa border by evening and set up for the night."

I climbed aboard and fired up the truck, turning back onto the highway and heading towards Iowa.

CHAPTER 13

We passed a number of communities on our way, many living, many more unlivable. For a long time, the standard policy was to simply burn down the buildings we weren't going to be able to maintain or use. Then someone got the bright idea to send in teams to strip the homes of useable materials, including building materials. We didn't have sawmills or manufacturers of construction materials. What we wound up with was warehouses of semi-used home repair goods that we could recycle into something we needed.

About three hours past the incident, I decided to pull off the road again. We were about an hour from Iowa, and I wanted to regroup a little. We were heading into unknown territory, and I wanted to make sure our heads were still in the game. With the driving, everyone had time to think, and I wanted to see if we had any new insights. I also had to go to the bathroom.

I pulled off the highway on Route 82 and headed south for a bit. North of us was the town of Geneseo, and they had weathered the storm pretty well. There had been some outbreaks, but since Springfield Armory made their guns there, they had managed to repel the invaders. We did some trading in the past and they were restarting the factory, last I heard.

South of the highway was farm country, though, and I wasn't going to go too far. There was a small building just a short way from the main road, and it was a good place to stop. The building looked like it had seen better days, as it was a low structure with a large awning to protect cars from the elements. No sign told what it might have been, and as I got out and stretched, I looked over at Charlie and shrugged.

Charlie returned the gesture and pointed at the small house down the road. "I think someone's living there, I'm going to see if I can talk to them."

"Good enough. We'll be here, figuring out where we will spend the night."

Sarah wandered to the other vehicle, and I walked over to the other side of the building to relieve myself. The building was a bit of a mystery, with closed curtains and a single door in the front. It didn't look like a church or a banquet hall, although it was big enough for either.

I finished up and walked back to the trucks, stopping halfway to wait for Charlie, who was jogging back from the house.

"Well?" I asked, stepping in alongside him.

"Bad news and worse news, depending on your point of view," Charlie said.

"Bad news first."

"They remember seeing our late friend a few weeks ago. He was running along the highway and didn't stop when they hailed him."

"That fits with what we already know, what's the worse news?"

"There may be a breach at East Moline. Zombie activity has been up recently."

I sighed. "Damn. Well, how are they fixed?"

"They're good, just waiting for winter to find the hole. It seems to be a trickle, so they've been handling it up to now." Charlie finished as we reached the trucks.

"Guess we have to keep an eye out, now. Great. What else could go wrong?" I asked, looking over the highway. I thought I saw something move, but nothing happened for a minute and I forgot it. I turned to the assembled faces in front of me.

"We're heading into Davenport, and will probably spend the night there. I think there's a hotel or something outside the containment zone," I said.

Sarah spoke up, "Any news, Charlie?"

Charlie shook his head. "Nothing new. Our friend came from the west, running hard. Nothing chasing him, but he was running jus the same."

"No vehicle?" Duncan asked.

"None. As far as anyone could determine, this guy was just running."

We all digested that for a bit. Charlie finished with his other news. "Probably a breach at East Moline, so we're on alert."

Duncan stretched. "Ahh, the good old days. Never quite leave us, do they?"

Rebecca pointed. "Not quite."

We all looked and saw a familiar lurching figure stumble into view under the highway. We had never seen this one specifically before, but we'd seen his type. Everyone tensed a bit, but I took the lead.

"Got it, just make sure he's alone," I said, drawing my .45 and advancing on the ghoul.

Charlie reached into the van and pulled out his AR, flicking off the safety and stepping into the bed of the truck. I kept walking, glancing down to make sure my gun was loaded and ready. I needn't have bothered, it had been so long since I had to check, but it never hurt. The one time I let it go would be the one time I got a click when I needed a bang.

About twenty yards up the road I stopped, and waited for the Z to get closer. He was about forty yards out, and while I could hit him, I might not kill him. As he got closer, I could see more details about him. His clothes were torn and shabby, yet I could see he was wearing the remnants of a business suit. His left arm swung a little too far out, balancing the rest of him, since he was missing half of his right arm. Bloodstains across the front of his body suggested his arm had been ripped off while he was alive and he had run for a bit before falling to the virus. Hell of a way to go.

At twenty yards or so, I lined up a shot, aiming just between his vacant eyes. One loud bang later and this dapper zombie was no more. I went over to the body and dragged it into the ditch. It was no fun cruising along and suddenly running over a dead zombie that someone had forgotten to move out of the way.

I walked back to the group and we mounted up. Sarah looked over at me and arched an eyebrow as we pulled back onto the highway.

"Yes, it felt better than the other guy," I said

"Just checking, sweetheart. Just checking."

CHAPTER 14

We got back onto I-80 and kept heading west. Out in the fields we could see a few wandering zombies, but since they were alone, we figured the locals could handle them. The ones that were closer to the highway we dispatched, with Charlie showing off his marksmanship. I was personally impressed with a five hundred yard shot he made, but Charlie tempered that when he told me that was the luckiest shot he had made so far.

I-80 turned north to go around the Quad Cities, and I decided to follow that route, instead of going the I-74 route. If there was a breach at East Moline, it had to be along this corridor, since the southern end of the city was blocked by a river. Also, the bridge at I-74 was impassable due to the car fence we had placed there a while ago.

Crossing the river brought a few memories back, some good, and some bad. We were officially in Iowa when we reached the other side, and I have to admit my apprehension level went a little higher. We were that much closer to whatever it was that was out there, and it wasn't a comforting thought.

Cruising down the I-74 highway, we got a good look at our previous handiwork. Our containment policy walled in dozens of subdivisions, and we could see hundreds of zombies milling about in the evening sun. Cars lined the edges of the highway, providing an additional layer of protection. For every zombie we saw, we knew there were ten inside the buildings. Something had evolved in the virus, and the zombies were staying away from the elements, hiding out indoors to keep from falling apart. They came out when they spotted you, or figured you could be eaten, and it was a nasty surprise when you thought a town was clear and suddenly a horde was chasing you down the street.

Just past the debris berms was the hotel I was looking for. It actually was the only one left outside the zone, so our choices were limited. I didn't feel like spending the night in the truck, and a secure location was a welcome sight. We had made several of these over the years as places for people to stop. I can't tell you how important it was to the psychological well-being of people to know they could travel and still feel safe.

The Abbey Hotel was a big brick building situated high on a hill. It actually used to be an abbey, but it had been renovated into a hotel/museum before the Upheaval. During the dark times, it had been used as a fortress against the zombies, and now it served as a resting spot on the main road.

We pulled into the parking lot just as the sun was settling into its evening descent. Long shadows played out over the landscape, and the frustrated groans of the zombies on the other side of the zones mingled with the calls of the hunting cats and dogs.

Duncan looked up at the Abbey and grimaced. "Creepy place. Are you sure there isn't a better hotel around here?"

I shook my head. "You burned them, remember? Back when you and Tommy took the river to the south?"

Duncan's shoulders slumped. "Oh, yeah." He brightened quickly. "Dibs on the corner room!" He grabbed his pack and scampered towards the hotel.

Sarah and I laughed, while Tommy managed a face palm holding two bags. Charlie just shook his head and Rebecca laughed.

We moved into the hotel, dropping our bags at the front door and joined Duncan in a quick sweep of the building. Everything checked out so we took the stairs to the rooms on the third floor. The fourth floor was the attic, and there wasn't anything up there.

As the sun slowly set, the light in the building turned from white to yellow to orange, changing the color of the walls from bright to melancholy. I left Sarah up in our room while I explored a little, finding a small room at the end of the hall blocked off by a piece of Plexiglas. The room contained a cot, a bedside table, a chair, and a tiny locker by the foot of the cot. A plaque informed me that this was a cell used by the nuns of the abbey. They each had their own room, and this one was preserved as part of the museum. A single homespun dress hung on a peg in the corner.

I wandered downstairs and passed by the lobby, moving my way into the dining area. The chairs and tables were long gone, probably used as firewood during the Upheaval. In the back of the dining room was a big door, and it was slightly ajar.

Curious, I went over and peeked inside. There was just enough light for me to see the small chapel contained within, with a tiny alter and several rows of pews. I stepped in and walked over to pews when the back door suddenly opened. I jumped at the intrusion, but relaxed when I saw it was Charlie.

"Spooked me there," I said, and chuckled when I saw my words had made Charlie jump.

"Jesus, don't do that," he said, walking over. "This place is creepy enough."

"What do you mean? I don't feel anything."

"How can you not?" Charlie asked. "This chapel is sitting on top of the kitchen."

"Gee, how terrifying," I said, looking at Charlie curiously.

"The kitchen is where the crypt used to be."

"Oh. Well, they're long gone, so we should be fine," I said, brushing off the chill I suddenly got.

"Yeah. I hope so. Let's get out of here." Charlie seemed genuinely spooked, which in itself was a wonder.

We made our way back to our rooms, and Sarah and I spent some quality time together before we drifted off to sleep.

CHAPTER 15

I awoke in the middle of the night to see Sarah sitting up in bed. The moonlight coming in through the window provided enough light for me to see she was staring at the ceiling, her hands gripping the blanket tightly. I reached out and touched her hand, and she nearly leaped out of bed.

"Jesus!" she cried, holding a hand to her chest and breathing heavily. I had never seen Sarah this scared before, and I was instantly wide awake.

"What's going on?" My threat level suddenly jumped and I was in battle mode instantly. I grabbed my pistol from the nightstand and got out of bed, the night sites on my gun oddly reassuring.

Sarah pointed at the ceiling. "Someone's walking around up there," she said.

I stood completely still and waited. After a minute, I could hear it plainly, too. The floor creaked in a rhythmic pattern, going around the edge of our room, and then stopping directly overhead. I aimed my gun at the ceiling, although I had no real reason to do so, and felt a distinct chill creep down my back.

The steps retreated and disappeared, and I looked at Sarah. She looked back at me and we both shrugged at the same time. I started towards the bed when I heard a footstep in the hallway. It wasn't overly loud, but loud enough that I wanted to investigate.

"What?" Sarah asked, seeing me turn towards the door.

"Someone's in the hallway." I whispered, moving to the small hallway between the door and the bathroom.

Sarah slipped out of bed and picked up her own gun, positioning herself on my side of the bed to give me backup if I needed it.

I reached the door and I could see a small band of moonlight under the door as the hallway was lit by a big window on the end of the hall. Just as I was starting to reach for the doorway, I froze. Two shadows, like someone's feet, blocked the moonlight and stopped in front of my door. The shadows then positioned themselves outside my door, like there was a person waiting to be let in.

For whatever reason, I could not open that door. I couldn't even put my hand on the doorknob. I just stood there with my gun ready and my hand outstretched. In the dim light, I could still see the shadow of someone standing outside my doorway. I brought my gun up but I knew instinctively it was only a comfort to me, and useless against whatever was in the hallway. I couldn't even bring myself to look through the peephole. I didn't want to see what was on the other side. Something was stopping me from looking, and I just stood there, staring at the door and the shadows.

"John?" Sarah whispered. "John? What is it?"

That broke the spell. The shadows disappeared from the doorway, and I found I could move again. I turned to Sarah and moved quickly back to the bed, placing my gun back on the nightstand. Sarah jumped in after me and held on tight.

"What was out there?" She asked.

I thought for a second. "If I had to guess, the nuns were making sure we stayed in bed."

In the morning, I awoke to a hammering on our door. Opening it, I found Charlie standing there with his bags in hand, nearly vibrating with energy.

"Ready to go? We're ready. We'll meet you down at the cars." With that, he was gone, moving quickly down the hall to the stairs.

Rebecca came after him and threw me a shrug, following Charlie to the parking lot. I shook my head and got dressed; throwing a wink to Sarah that put a blush on her beautiful cheeks as she dressed.

Downstairs I bumped into Tommy and Duncan, and after a quick conference confirmed that they had no strange things happen to them. They were curious about my experience, and I gave them the short version of it, leaving out the part of me being scared stiff.

Walking out to the truck, I tossed my pack in the back and climbed in next to Sarah.

"You talk to Rebecca at all?" I asked as I fired up the truck. Charlie had the van already warm.

"Mmm Hmmm."

"And?"

"Charlie looked into the hallway last night."

I had a heck of a time keeping up with him as we sped away from the Abbey Hotel.

CHAPTER 16

We moved away from Bettendorf and back onto the main highway. I was anxious to get to the source of the problem and report back as soon as I could. If something was headed towards the population centers of Illinois, I wanted to get ahead of it, especially since my children might be right in its path. Jake had come with us on the campaign against the zombies, and Aaron had been born in the middle of the fights, but I didn't want to think about my family being in harm's way while I was away.

I-80 was still very quiet in the early hours, but we would likely see some trucks as the day progressed. There was a lot more movement these days than there had been in the past, but it was still limited. People stayed close to where they were safe, and only idiots like us wandered off the reservation on a regular basis.

While I drove, Sarah looked over the maps, trying to get some sort of read on what we were facing, and trying to predict where the best insertion point might be.

"If this mess is moving towards the center of the state, maybe we should just wait for it? No, then we might be weeks out here, and for all we know we might be passed by." She spoke out loud to herself when she was musing, and it was hard to follow when I wasn't sure when she was talking to me.

"What?"

"Hmm, what sweetie?"

"You say something?" I asked.

"No sorry, just thinking out loud, you know me."

"Talk to me, we're about six hours out of where we need to turn south," I said, checking my rear view for the van. It was steady behind me about ten car lengths back, and Charlie looked as bored as I was. While Iowa was pretty, it was monotonous.

"Well, I'm looking at the map, and we have some possibilities. The first town not reporting in is here, and the last one is here. Given the distance, I'd have to say the problem is on foot, moving roughly faster than a walk, but not fast enough for a car." Sarah squinted at the map. "What I don't get is the lack of response. How can something like this happen and no one report it? I mean no one."

I shrugged, causing the truck to swerve slightly. "Couldn't say. But here's my thought. I want to go to the first town that go hit, and check things out. If it's something that changes the war, then we bug out and prepare our defenses. If it's something we can fight, we can follow it and take it unawares. If we wait for it, like you mumbled back there, then it might pass us by and we're out here when we should be elsewhere."

Sarah smacked me on the arm for my comment, but nodded to herself. "Makes a kind of sense. If we follow it, at least we know we're on the right track and can deal with it for sure, then guessing when it might come by." She frowned at her maps. "Looking at these towns, I wonder what happened to the people who came before us."

I thought about the man I had shot in that army / navy store. "I don't know. I just don't know."

CHAPTER 17

About noon, we pulled off the road at the little town of Adair. According to the map, the road headed down towards where we wanted to go. In normal times, we would have travelled to Interstate 29, but that road was closed to us. When we decided to clear the roads, some had to be bypassed, and that was one of them. So we were on side roads until we reached our destination.

That was fine with me. I was always a country traveler anyway. I always wanted to see the land I passed through, not just catch glimpses out of the corner of my eye as I blew past.

This also served the purpose of checking out the lay of the land before we faced whatever it was that was causing the problem out here. I hoped we could find out from a distance, but in my heart of hearts, I knew we were going to hit it head on, and we weren't going to like it.

At the town of Anita, we stopped to talk to some locals and filled them in on the situation. They said they hadn't seen anything out of the ordinary, but they would check in more frequently now. They were well situated for defense, being near a large lake and forest preserve. All they had to do was get in one of the numerous boats that lined the shore and they were safe.

At Wiota, we ran into much of the same, a community that had weathered the storm fairly well. Wiota was a small farming town that was used to being self-reliant, so the end of the world wasn't much of a concern. They promised to send out a contact report and let the powers that be know we had been in the area and still hadn't seen anything out of the ordinary.

We turned further south after skirting the town of Atlantic. That particular town had managed to survive the initial Upheaval, but an errant traveler had started a fire in a fake fireplace and scorched three quarters of the town. The people who had lived there scattered to the other towns and left Atlantic to ruin.

At Lewis, we turned to Route 6 and followed that to Oakland. In Oakland, you would never have known anything had ever happened to their world. The streets were clear, the homes were tidy, and people were everywhere going about their daily duties. It was a very nice place, and I almost felt out of place when I stopped at the sheriff's office to let him know what we were up to.

Two deputies, dressed in civilian gear but wearing badges, sized me up as I got out of the truck, and their eyes widened when Charlie and Duncan stepped out of the van. We were dressed for battle, and I caught one deputy trying not to be too obvious about putting his hand near his gun.

"Afternoon, gents. Your boss around?" I asked, figuring this shouldn't take too long.

The taller of the two deputies answered. "He's out at his house, he don't come in till later. Anything I can help you with?"

"Just wanted to relay a warning, that's all," I said.

"Warning?" Both deputies stiffened slightly. "About what?"

I related to the two of them who I was and what I was doing out here. Both of them said they hadn't heard of any problems, but now that I had mentioned it, they hadn't seen anybody from the southern part of the state in a while.

"All right, well, we'll keep going, and if anything and I mean, anything is out of the ordinary, lock up tight and spread the word." I warned.

"You think it's another outbreak?" Asked the shorter deputy. He glanced around, as if he expected to see a zombie roll out from under the bushes.

"Wish I could tell you, son. Take it easy and keep your eyes open," I said as I climbed back aboard the truck.

We rolled out of Oakland and ten miles further west we turned south again towards Glenwood. I will admit I was getting nervous, mostly from the astounding lack of information we had regarding this whole mess. Part of me just wished something would happen. Anything that might give me a clue as to what we were facing. Hell, I would have welcomed even a former campsite from another group just to look for a few clues.

At Treynor, we stopped and stretched our legs. This town was wide open and completely abandoned. During the Upheaval, these people had gone to Council Bluffs for protection and to help defend the city there from the hordes of zombies that lined the river at Omaha. Hundreds of people lost their lives defending the two bridges keeping away the Zs, and to this day, they still have men manning the bridges, making sure the defenses don't fall. The people of the surrounding communities are fully aware of the sacrifices the people at Council Bluffs have made, and are appropriately grateful.

Most of the houses were nearly buried in tall grass and unkempt bushes. We passed dozens of homes that were in severe disrepair, and some that had burned down. I pulled over at the corner of Eyberg and Main, and Sarah nodded to me absently. I knew she was starting to feel things as well, not the least of which was the nagging uncertainty.

Charlie came over from the van while Tommy and Duncan wandered off to find a place to go to the bathroom. I suggested just pick a nearby bush, but they must have been sensitive souls given their response.

"How far?" Charlie asked, looking over the building we parked next to. It was Anderson's Service, but what it serviced I couldn't say.

I stretched a bit. "By the map, we should be there in about an hour. I figure we'd get closer to Council Bluffs and head south, come in from the north."

"Good enough. I think we can rule out rogue group, by the way."

"How so?"

"I figured someone would have heard about it by now, and our two deputies back there seemed bored enough to check up on anything out of the ordinary," Charlie said, taking a look into the big brick building.

I had to admit he was probably right. Groups that try to establish themselves tended to blast through the countryside pretty quickly, and after a brief flare up, were typically handled and quieted. We had a run in up in Montana with a group but when it turned out their leader was an old friend of ours, it worked out pretty well.

"Well, we'll see things for ourselves in a bit, and go from there." I glanced over my shoulder to see Tommy trotting up to us.

"Hey. Duncan climbed the water tower for a look around and he says there's a zombie stream to the south of us, heading this way," Tommy said.

"All right. Tell him to come down and we'll have a look. Did he say how long?" I remarked, my hand straying to my sidearm.

"Couldn't make a determination, all he said was it was on its way. The upside was it was close to a road."

That helped. It was a pain in the neck to deal with a zombie stream in the middle of nowhere. Zombie streams are what we called the long lines of zombies that trailed away from population centers. Typically, one would get the notion to roam, another would notice, and so on until several were strung out in a long line from wherever they came from. The bigger the city, the longer the stream. We had one that went for fifteen miles once.

"Let's go. Maybe this is the start of an explanation." I waved on Sarah and Rebecca, and we hopped back into the vehicles to go take a look.

CHAPTER 18

I let Charlie take the lead, since Duncan had seen the stream and knew where it was. We drove out of town and headed south on a county road. The van turned right almost immediately and followed a farm road for a about a mile. I looked over at Sarah as the van took another turn south and went down an oil and gravel road that connected several small farms in the area. I knew from experience these farm roads were typically a mile long, so we would find the next intersection in a minute or two.

"Do you think Duncan was seeing things?" Sarah asked as she stopped herself from hitting the ceiling when we went over a particularly large bump.

"Not Duncan. He's a goof, but he's never wrong about Zs," I said, steering around a large pothole. The van in front of me swerved and swayed, and I wondered if Charlie was trying to hit the most number of potholes.

We reached the next intersection and went west again, turning south once more at another farm road. Sarah pointed out that there was a small town in this area, which explained why there might have been a drift.

Suddenly, Charlie hit the brakes, and I was glad of my seatbelt when I slid to a stop behind him.

"That was fun," I said as I climbed out of the truck and grabbed my carbine from the area behind the seat. Sarah did the same and I pulled out my pickaxe from the truck bed. Sarah hefted a small spear, and then nodded. The spear was one Duncan had brought home one day. It was four feet of pole, then two feet of sharpened, pointed steel. It cut as well as it poked. I'd use one myself, but my pick was just so comfortable.

As we went to the side of the van, it suddenly opened and very deadly looking people spilled out. Duncan came first, followed by Tommy, then Rebecca and Charlie. Everyone bristled with weapons, and I smiled as I saw the big sword strapped to Duncan's back.

Duncan noticed the smile and returned with one of his own. "You'll see, it will replace the gun, eventually."

I liked to needle Duncan about his weapon choices, but truth be known it made a lot of sense. Medieval weapons were making a comeback in the war on the zombies, and a lot of people trained with them these days.

"Where's the stream?" I asked Charlie since I assumed that was why he stopped.

"Saw the head over...there." He pointed to the south and sure enough, a stumbling form was headed this way. In the distance, more could be seen, moving in a slow shamble towards us.

"All right. You all know what to do. Charlie, you take number one, I'll head off for number two. No guns, in case there's bigger problems around. The rest of you spread out and take them as they come." Nodding heads and grim faces went off to battle. In a situation like this, we tended to let the zombies come to us and kill them. If we ran out to them, we had to come all the way back to our transportation.

We went to the other side of the van and I walked forward as Charlie went to meet our first customer. It was a short man, with blood steaks all over his head and arms. His eyes scanned all of us before they locked on Charlie, and by that time, it was too late. Charlie planted one of his tomahawks in the Z's head and sent him to the ground. The second one on line, a tall female, stumbled somewhat quickly towards me as I walked her way. My pick was already in my hand, and I dodged her arms as she lunged. I slammed the head of the pick into her knee, sending her crashing to the ground. Her reaching hand caught my pant leg, but I was already in the downswing of my killing stroke. The pointed end of the pick cracked her skull and kept her on the ground for good.

The rest of the team spread out and waited, and naturally, the zombies came to us. Big, little, old and not so old shambled to the killing zone, eager to try their luck at the succulent morsels just out of reach. We took turns killing them, and ran out after about fifteen zombies had bitten the dust.

We cleaned our weapons and piled back into the vehicles, since where there was a zombie stream, chances were there was a zombie town nearby. The nearest one that was in the general direction of the source of the stream was Mineola, so we headed that way.

Mineola was an extremely small town literally in the middle of nowhere, so it was a something of a surprise to see any zombies hanging around out there, but as we pulled into the outskirts of town that's exactly what we saw. There were about three dozen zombies wandering about, and when the first ones spotted us and started groaning, the rest soon joined in.

I drove slowly around the town, following the convenient road that kept to the outskirts. When it turned into the town, I kept going, making sure the zombies were able to keep us in sight.

"Look for a place to take care of them all at once, will you?" I asked Sarah. I had to keep an eye on the road, since there was more debris than I expected there to be. This town had been active, and by the looks of things, there seemed to be a lot of chaos about.

"I'll try, but these trees aren't making things any easier," Sarah said, sitting straighter in her seat and looking in every direction she could.

The radio came to life. "What's the plan?" Charlie asked.

I grabbed the handset. "Looking for a place to bottle them up or trap them in."

"Good luck. This place is smaller than our dock back home."

I turned down Main Street, and Sarah smacked me on the arm. "There! That building!"

I looked. It was a long, low building with windows up near the roofline. Perfect. I pulled the truck in to the back of the structure and ran towards the front. The feed store had a single doorway, and was open all the way to the back. A second structure was attached which I presumed was the warehouse for goods.

Charlie was beside me and as we stood by the door, the first group of zombies that had followed our vehicles walked into view. I waved my arms and they lurched a little faster in our direction. I took the time to look them over and something struck me as odd, but I couldn't put a finger on what it was. Something just wasn't right, but I didn't have time to put it through my problem-solving process.

CHAPTER 19

"You want the front or the back?" Charlie asked, hefting a 'hawk in each hand and looking very grim.

"I'll take the back. Just get out of the way this time, all right?" I said as I went into the building, dodging piles of feed sacks.

"You act like I'm the only one who's done dumb things." Charlie called, perturbed.

"I wasn't the one who managed to trap myself behind a door for two hours." I yelled back, but Charlie didn't hear me. He was waving his arms and making noise, trying to make sure as many zombies came towards the door as possible. I stayed about three-quarters of the way into the building, ready to start calling the zombies in further to trap them in the building. I positioned myself between the piles of fertilizer and pesticide, guaranteed to make my tomatoes the best ever.

As I looked to the front door, I saw Charlie duck inside and hide behind the big swinging door. Five seconds later, a zombie made its way into the store, and I immediately banged my pick and my knife together to get its attention. I didn't want it to sniff out Charlie's hiding spot and cause some serious problems. The zombie's head snapped up. I could almost see its eyes narrow and its lips peel back from its teeth as it marched towards me. Behind it, several more zombies streamed in through the door, and I was going to cut this close in order to get as many zombies in here as possible before Charlie could get back outside and secure the door. If there were stragglers, Duncan and Tommy were likely hiding nearby to lend a hand. Sarah and Rebecca were probably getting some kind of firebomb ready to light this building up.

A few more bangs and a small stand on top of a pile of feed to get as many focused on me as possible allowed Charlie to dart outside and close the door behind him. I took that as my cue and ran towards the back door ready to get out and set this place on fire.

Great plans typically are designed around the guiding principle that everything will go right. Good plans have backups for the inevitable screw up that twists things sideways. Lousy plans are doomed to failure, usually because of some sort of oversight or cruddy planning.

I evaluated my plan for evacuating the building when I pushed on the emergency bar on the back door and walked right into the door. I shook my head and tried the door again, which stubbornly resisted my efforts to open it. Looking at the door, I saw it was opening, but it was secured in place by a latch and very effective padlock.

"Oh, shit." I didn't have much else to say, and it would have been a wasted effort anyway.

I turned around and saw the zombies had covered the distance fairly well and the first two were going to reach me in just a few seconds. I whipped out my pistol and quickly fired two shots, knocking over the nearest zombies. The shots seemed to galvanize the rest into charging the rear of the building, which had the effect of making me very nervous.

To make things worse, there was a pounding on the back door and Sarah's voice, which seemed very far away. "John? John? John! Duncan, help!"

I didn't have time to talk. I needed to move. I ducked away to the left, skipping around pallets of feed and pesticide, pausing for an instant to ventilate a nearby Z. I bolted for the front of the building, figuring to buy some sort of time and maybe get out the way Charlie did.

The front of the building was better lit thanks to the abundance of windows, but that didn't make the zombies look any better. Jumping the checkout counter I slammed into the door, only to realize the damn thing had been secured on the outside by Charlie and he never made a mistake when it came to locking up Z's.

"Damn, damn, damn," I said to myself as the groans from the formerly living inhabitants worked their way through the displays towards the front.

All right. Plan B. I stepped to the right and when the zombies worked over that way, I shifted my aim and killed four on the left side. Running through the small opening that gave me I ran to the middle of the store, shot another small zombie that was missing an ear. His companion, an old woman that bared gums at me, went down with a shot in the eye.

I reloaded and ran back to the rear, staying to the far right again. I crouched and took aim at the padlock on the door, and shot the hell out of it, but of course, the stupid thing stayed on. I fired again and this time the thing broke, but the zombies had reached me so I shot four more on the left side. Darting through the opening, I ran back to the front, and waited for the zombies to pick up the chase again.

They didn't disappoint, and I used the same technique again, thinning the herd a little more. Running as fast as I could to the back, I ripped the padlock out of the latch and threw it aside.

"Coming out!" I yelled and shoved the door open, ducking as three rifles covered me. I slammed the door closed and hollered at Tommy. "I need a wedge!" The door thumped loudly and I could feel many dead hands pounding on the other side. It was only a matter of time before the press of bodies activated the push bar and opened the door.

"Got it!" Tommy ran up with a hammer and small metal shim. He pounded the shim into the space between the door and the frame, sealing the exit.

I fell on the ground, and breathed heavily. Sarah knelt down next to me and put her hand on my back. I winked at her and stood up, pulling her close for a grateful kiss.

"Thanks very much," I said over the noise of the pounding corpses.

"What happened?" Charlie asked. "You were supposed to be out right after me."

"Padlock on the rear door," I said. "Didn't see it when I first checked the exit. My bad."

"Your bad nearly took you out, pal," Duncan said, crossing his arms.

"Ease up," I said. "I had enough room to make runs back and forth. Thanks for securing the front door so well," I said to Charlie.

Charlie scowled but Rebecca spoke up. "It's done, you're all right, let's get it lit."

"Go for it," I said. I walked back to the truck and pulled out a box of ammo. I replaced the rounds I had used and checked the rest of my mags. Sarah came over and out a hand on my arm.

"You okay? You seem like you have something to prove, and are willing to risk your friendship with Charlie to do it." Sarah's green eyes looked into mine and I slumped slightly.

I shook my head. "Just tired of screwing up this trip, you know? I never saw the padlock because I never checked the door. I just assumed it would open."

Sarah nodded. "Well, it had to happen sometime."

"What's that?"

"The great John Talon made a mistake." Sarah's eyes twinkled.

"That's not funny," I said.

"No, it's human. Welcome to the club. Try not to get yourself killed or you will piss me off." Sarah pulled me down to kiss my cheek and walked over to the building where Duncan was prepping a can of gas to use on the building.

I watched her walk off and finally laughed. I put the box of ammo back and saw Sarah lean over and whisper something to Rebecca. I could only imagine what it was.

Duncan disappeared for a minute, and then came running back, jumping in the van.

"Let's go! I've never rigged one like that before so I don't know for sure what it's going to do!" he yelled.

That was enough for the rest of us. Usually when Duncan rigged something, it was a good idea to check to make sure you had nothing loose on you that might blow off, and preferably had a strong handhold on something solid. The next best thing was to get away as quickly as possible.

We dove into the vehicles and sped away, trying to get as much distance as we could. After racing out of town, we stopped and looked back. Nothing had happened, so I was wondering if the trap had been a bust.

"Where's the boom? Usually when you touch something, it goes boom." Tommy asked as Duncan scanned the sky for smoke.

"I'm not sure. I rigged it like I normally do, but maybe it landed on something that put it out, or...."

Whatever Duncan was going to say was drowned out in a loud whoompf, followed by a huge fatooom! The center of the town suddenly erupted in flame and a pillar of flame, debris, and body parts lanced skyward in an effort to defy gravity. We could actually see the shock wave, and staggered as it hit us.

I couldn't resist. I tried, but I failed.

"Think you used enough dynamite there, Butch?" I said.

CHAPTER 20

Duncan was wide eyed at his handiwork, and Charlie was the second to speak.

"The fertilizer probably did it. Pretty cool, though," he said.

"Well, that ought to attract any strays and let everyone know we're here," I said. Charlie looked over at me and Duncan looked hurt, but I clarified when I said, "If someone comes investigating, that will give us the edge because we can see them coming. If no one shows up, for sure it's not a rogue group."

Several nods greeted me and Charlie walked over, shifting his head for a private talk. I obliged, figuring I owed him an apology for acting like an ass earlier.

"What's up?" I asked, starting the ball, looking at the smoke rising to the sky. Several other buildings had been set on fire, so this one was going to be big.

"Not too much. Did you notice anything about our zombie friends?"

I thought about it. "They seemed pretty fresh, now that you mention it." I thought a little more." Their clothes were in pretty good shape, too."

"Didn't notice the clothes." Charlie reflected. "Did you notice there weren't any kids with them?"

"Now that you mention it, no, I didn't see any. That's odd." It was, too. This far after the Upheaval, kids were making a serious leap in the population. I attributed it to people taking the responsibility to get the world jump started, but Duncan would always say it was because there wasn't anything on television to keep people's hands off each other.

"What do you think it means?" Charlie asked.

"Don't know yet, but I have a feeling it's to the south of us."

"Yeah me too."

"Charlie?"

"Don't mention it. You got out. We're good. If you'd bought it, I'd be feeling bad."

"Thanks man."

We went back to the group and boarded our truck and van. We had one more stop to make before we could try and figure out what was going on. The only thing we pulled away from this town was it had been recently alive and there were no children here. If it was a rogue group, then they were using zombies as weapons and stealing children for who knows what purpose.

If that was true, then they'd better find a place to hide before Charlie was unleashed on them.

Five miles south of what was left of Mineola, we stopped at the intersection of County Highway 45 and Gaston Avenue. There were five homes around this little intersection, and it would have been easy to believe the troubles of the world never touched this place. However, the homes were abandoned, locked up and left, without vehicles in the garages or barns. I didn't disturb the homes, hoping that someday the owners might return to their little piece of heaven. The grass was long, as it was everywhere, and the fields were returning to the days before the plow, but the scene was still nice. Sarah pointed out that on the three mailboxes on the east side of the road all had the same name on the mailboxes. I guess around here people really don't get too far from the homestead.

We took a moment to eat some lunch, and then we all gathered around the truck bed to look at the map. The towns we were concerned with were circled in black, and I knew everyone was concerned that it looked to be spreading east, whatever it was. The only thing that was a comfort was the thought that if it were zombies, they would be stopped at the Mississippi River.

The maps we had were pretty large, being little more than state road maps, but they had nearly all of the roads save for the county back roads that only locals and former county police officers knew about. We didn't have any of those handy so we had to do what we always did and just wing it.

"All right. We're about a mile or so from where the whole mystery started, so we need to figure out how we're going to approach this. We know there's zombie activity around here thanks to the little episode back north. Since we haven't seen anyone on the road to investigate Duncan's handiwork, I'm going to assume this town is dead. Based on the map info, there may be anywhere from three to five thousand zombies in here," I said.

"Any good news?" Tommy asked.

"None that I can think of, except this isn't an extermination mission. We go to take a look, try to figure out what's going on, see what the threat might be, then get back to Leport. If there's something on the way to our families, I want to be in front of it, not chasing it." I explained.

Charlie nodded. "Okay, but what if we can't figure out what happened here, or what happened to the teams sent out filled this way?"

I pointed to the map. "We move to the next town and search for clues. Nothing else we can do."

Sarah spoke up. "If we do that, then we're not standing in the way of what might be moving around, but coming up behind it."

Rebecca nodded. "Best way to ambush whatever it is."

Charlie looked at his wife, then at me. I shrugged.

"You trained her, pal."

Charlie blocked the playful punch Rebecca tossed at him. "That's what scares me," he said.

"All right, we're going in slow. Radios on and keep them low. I want everyone's eyes looking for anything that might give us a clue as to why these towns are falling off the grid." I rolled up the map and we all separated to get our gear ready. I filled up my magazines to capacity and added three more to my belt. I loosened the zipper on the top of my backpack, so I could get at the tomahawk in there. I had to admit Charlie had a good thing with his, and it had impressed me enough over the years to get one of my own. While his were more traditional, mine had a polymer handle and grip, and the blade of a spike on the other end balanced the weapon. It was light, sharp, and awesomely deadly. I couldn't throw it nearly as well as Charlie could, but I was getting better. In a major fight, though, I would revert to my long handled pickaxe, which rode in its accustomed place.

Sarah was focused on her gear, which looked better on her anyway. She kept things light, preferring movement to brute force. Her weapon of choice was a spike on a long handle. Sarah liked to poke her zombies on top of their heads, and if they needed finishing off, she had her long knife. She had gone back to her Ruger .22 for a sidearm for this trip, and carried my old GSG-5 for a long gun. We had proven time and again the .22 was effective on zombies, and Sarah was nothing short of lethal.

She teased me again how she could carry ten times as much ammo as I could and still have it weigh the same, and in private, I wondered sometimes why the hell I used a .45. But the upside was anything I shot with it stayed very dead.

We regrouped and moved into position. From what I could remember, Glenwood was a town that spread out mostly north of a small river. The river was no obstacle to zombies, being only a foot or two deep, but it was fast enough in places to slow them down. Most of the town was subdivision, with the newer parts on the far north.

As we drove slowly into the outskirts, it was as if we were driving into the past. Empty houses with open doors and bits of dirty rag hanging on mailboxes spoke volumes. Here and there, a skeleton lay in the ditch or near a doorway. Some had head trauma we could see, others were just sprawled about. Sarah pointed to a house on the right that had nearly twenty skeletons scattered about the front lawn.

We didn't see any moving dead, so we pressed further into town. On Linn Street, we passed an elementary school that looked intact, except for a single open door on the north side. A quick glance showed it could have been used as a decent shelter, since the windows were high and the front doors were solid with only a small window on them. The only thing that looked weird was the flattened grass leading away from the building from the open door.

CHAPTER 21

We continued south until we reached Fourth Street. There was a zombie barrier here, letting us know the area further south should have living people in it. I looked over at Sarah and she just shook her head. I nodded, because I had the same feeling. The barrier was a three-foot trench dug into the ground, with the dirt piled on the opposite side. It gave the defenders an effective five-foot barrier to the zombies, but it also put the zombies at nearly perfect killing level.

I got out of the truck and walked over to the ditch. There were quite a few dead things in the ditch, and not all of them were permanently dead. When they saw me, three of them started in my direction, stumbling over corpses and other obstacles.

I was about to pull out the pick when Duncan stepped up beside me. "Allow me," he said, pulling his sword out of its sheath. It was a big two-handed affair, with a long double-sided blade.

"Oh, by all means," I said, bowing out of the way. I winked at Sarah and nodded at Tommy, who was shouldering his rifle to give Duncan backup.

Duncan stepped up to the first ghoul, who was reaching for him with skeletal hands, both of which were missing fingers. Duncan swung quickly, neatly severing the Z's head from its neck and cutting off the hands for good measure.

The second zombie took a quick stab through the eye that still left a foot of steel coming out of the back of its skull, and the last took a cut right at eye level, completely removing the top of the corpse's head.

All three kills took less than ten seconds, and I looked back at Charlie and Tommy with raised eyebrows. Tommy just nodded and put away his rifle, while Charlie was taking a serious look at Duncan's sword. I had to admit, that was a pretty effective and silent method of killing zombies.

I stepped over a zombie that was sprawled across the ditch, and climbed the small berm. I hoped to see some activity of the living, but I wasn't hoping for much. As it was, I was hoping for too much.

"What do you see, John?" Sarah asked.

"Nothing," I said.

"What's nothing?"

"That's what I mean. There's nothing here. The homes are busted into, and I can see some zombie activity further down the way, but I other than that, there's nothing living here." I hopped off the berm and crossed back to the group.

"How do you want to play it?" Tommy asked.

"We need to know why this town is suddenly dead, and how is it moving from town to town. Obviously, it's the virus. But how is it getting here?" My big fear was the virus had become airborne, and that's just what I was suggesting now.

"Well, we won't learn anything here. Sarah and Rebecca, you two take the truck and the van and get across to the other side. We'll take a stroll and meet you on the other side," I said, bracing myself for the onslaught.

"What! Hey, wait a minute..."

"Are you kidding? John..."

I raised my hands. "No joking. We need coverage from the other side, and you two are the best rifle shots we have. If we need a lane to escape through, I need someone who can put a round where they're supposed to, and not through someone's leg." I didn't look at Duncan, but I didn't have to. I knew he was cringing.

The ladies jumped into the vehicles and drove off, mollified, while the rest of us felt ourselves up for weapons and ammo.

I looked over at Charlie, who had decided to arm himself early with his twin tomahawks. "Care to be a distraction today?" I said as I pulled my long knife and trench 'hawk of my own.

"Love to." Charlie replied, rolling his shoulders and popping his neck.

"You two, give us ten minutes. The houses are yours. Check as many as you can, don't bother with locked ones, and see if you can figure out what the hell is going on," I said to Tommy and Duncan, who both nodded.

I took a deep breath, stepped over to the other side of the ditch, and climbed over the berm. Charlie was right beside me, and with a final stretch of his big arms, he nodded.

"Let's go."

We started off at a brisk pace, ignoring the groans and shuffling that came from the homes and side yards. We weren't there to fight them all. We were just there to herd them along like little lethal pied pipers.

There was a risk to what we were doing. If enough zombies ahead of us heard the ruckus and started closing in, we could find ourselves between two large groups. If that happened, we had to make a break for a house to hole up in until the cavalry arrived. That was a reason not to start shooting.

We also had to make sure we cleared a path for ourselves and make sure Tommy and Duncan weren't left high and dry. The goal was to herd the zombies along, freeing up the houses for inspection.

The good news was there wasn't a lot of zombie activity in the street itself. Had there been a good number of the ghouls, we never would have used this method. The bad news was we couldn't just take a leisurely walk. Tommy and Duncan were going to have to do a hurried search for clues.

Charlie and I walked about a block before the zombies started shuffling our way. We stayed ahead of them through a combination of walking and jogging. Our kills were going to have to be fast, and it sucked not to be able to shoot.

"On your side, fast stepper," Charlie said.

"Got it. I'll let him reach the street," I said, readying my weapons. Part of me wanted to get another tomahawk, but the crew would never let me live it down, after I had extolled the virtues of my pick for so many years.

The zombie had long legs, which gave it speed, and was recently dead, as evidenced by its lack of grey color and abundance of blood all over it. I stepped forward, and when it came within reach, I slammed the spike end of my 'hawk into the top of its head. A quick jerk got it out, as the Z collapsed, and I waited for Charlie to catch up.

Behind us, there was about thirty zombies, stumbling out of homes and shambling over yards. They were about twenty yards away from us, and over by the berm, I could see two heads popping up, checking to see if it was okay to start looking into homes.

"Let's lead them on." I walked backwards for a bit, keeping an eye on our friends, making sure there weren't any real fast ones needing to be dealt with. For the most part, it was your standard horde, except this one was still relatively new.

On the right, Charlie saw a couple heading our way, and a quick trajectory calculation put them ahead of us at the wrong time. He jogged over to the first, smashing it across the head with his first hit, finishing it with his second. The second zombie, a smaller woman, reached for him and he used his free weapon to crack her in the temple, dropping her on top of her companion.

I had kept walking, and joined him at the street. "So far so good. Duncan and Tommy just split up to check the houses."

"Don't think they're going to find much," Charlie said, scanning the road ahead.

"Neither do I, but I think we need to keep an eye on what we don't find as much as what we do," I said.

"Explain."

I walked over to a yard first and kicked a zombie teen in the chest, knocking him to the ground. His throat was torn out, and his shirt was drenched in old blood, but his eyes still had that 'whatever' look to them. I planted my axe head between those eyes and closed them for good. Stepping back into the street I explained to Charlie what I meant.

"If we look into fifty homes, and see that everything is just fine, but the cabinets are bare, the logical conclusion is the lack of food tells us someone was there before us and took supplies," I said.

Charlie nodded. "Okay, I see where you're going. So we need to look at what is not in front of us to have an idea of what might be." Charlie thought for a second. "Nope, just managed to confuse myself. Try again."

"Hold on, we have a problem," I said. In front of us were about fifteen zombies, and they were all in the street. We couldn't take them all on before the ones behind us would flank our rear. Time to get speedy.

"I'll run left, you go right. Meet you on the other side of those houses."

"Got it, go."

Charlie and I split and headed in opposite directions. I went to the left and ducked between two homes, running through the backyard and up the other side yard. Charlie was running right for me from the other side and as we passed through the front yards, we both yelled to get the Z's attention that had started to follow us to the back. We needed them in the front, because Tommy and Duncan, who were still sneaking along in the rear, would have had them to deal with if they were hanging out by the barbecues.

CHAPTER 22

Back in the street, we paused to catch our breath.

"How much further?" Charlie asked, moving south again.

"Not much, I can see the business district from here. According to the map, the girls should be on the other side of Coolidge Street," I said looking for the nearest street sign.

"Again, how far?" Charlie actually sounded winded.

"Three blocks, if this is 2nd Street." I looked back and nearly jumped. Four zombies had outpaced the rest and they were about ten feet from us.

"Shit! Back!" I shouted, whipping up my axe. The upstroke caught the zombie under the ear. Unfortunately, it was a larger gentleman who was missing half his face, and the blade lodged in his head at a bad angle, doing little to kill him. I let go of the handle and backpedalled, pulling out my pickaxe and finding some firmer ground to stand on. The second Z, a smaller ghoul whose jaw had been ripped off, stumbled forward and died as I planted my pick in his head. I dodged the clumsy grab of the big guy, and kicked him in the hip as he went past. He tumbled to the ground and as he bent over to get up, I cracked his skull with my weapon. I pulled out the 'hawk from his throat, chastising myself for trying for a kill in such a difficult spot.

Looking over at Charlie, I saw him finish off his second and wipe the blades off on the zombie's bathrobe. The horde behind us was a lot closer, and unless we wanted to get into a serious fight, we'd have to get moving.

"Let's get some distance, shall we?" I said jogging away from the groaning mass.

"Grand idea, right behind you," Charlie said, dragging his corpses to the street to try and trip up a few zombies. Mine were already there, so it might give us a few seconds.

We jogged for a block, and then waited. The houses thinned out as the streets gave way to businesses, so the possibility of attacks was smaller. Still, we'd been surprised before, so we waited in the open intersection of Linn and Sharp streets. Across the way, a large building rose up out of the grass, and the sign on the side told me it used to be a YMCA. To the south of us, a block away, was Coolidge Street, and I could see the defensive berm, as it wound its way around the southern portion of the safe zone.

"All righty then. Any sign of the Banana Brothers?" I asked, scanning the area, looking for any signs of activity. The town was pretty intact, for all general purposes, and would make a good place to live, barring whatever had wiped it out.

"Yeah, they just scooted out of the last houses. We'd better distract the masses," Charlie said. The zombies were about fifty yards away, and were surprisingly quiet. Very few were actually groaning, and part of me wondered if that had anything to do with what we were dealing with here.

I took out my trench 'hawk and banged the head of it and my pickaxe together. Charlie did the same, and the loud pinging was like a dog whistle to the Z's. They zeroed in on the sound and I swear they shuffled just a little faster. Several zombies that were drifting off at the edges of the group re-focused and joined the horde.

Around the outer edges of the horde, Tommy and Duncan came streaking past, surprising the zombies and causing them to redouble their efforts to get to us. It was a hopeless cause, since we just turned and ran away. I wasn't worried about this town being full of zombies, since they had managed to seal themselves in when they had originally sealed the zombies out. I take wins where I find them.

CHAPTER 23

We crossed the berm and ditch, walking past a plumbing supply warehouse and following Coolidge into the heart of the business district. At Vine Street, we reconnected with the women, and took a moment to burn off the zombie gunk on our weapons.

"Anything?" Sarah asked, looking over the four of us for any wounds or trauma.

"Don't know yet. Haven't really sat down to talk yet," I said, taking a drink out of a canteen.

"Well, tell me you love me," Sarah said mysteriously.

I looked at her strangely. "All, right. I love you."

"We may have something on the cause of this mess." She smiled at Rebecca.

I looked over at Rebecca and she looked at Charlie.

Charlie shrugged. "Okay, I love you, too. What's going on?"

Sarah pulled out the map. "Rebecca and I found the communications center for this town, and before you ask, yes, it works, and no, we didn't contact anyone. We figured having no new information was no better than no information, so we waited. Second, we may have an idea as to the source."

That shook me. "Really? What is it?" I asked.

Sarah shook her head. "We're guessing, so we need to put together anything you guys found."

Tommy put his hands up in a surrender gesture. "On my side of the street, I found homes that had been lived in up until recently, and there was a lot of blood in the bedrooms. That was it. Weapons were left in the open, and nothing of use to a survivor was taken."

Duncan nodded. "It was the same on my side of the street. Lots of blood in bedrooms and on beds, and nothing taken."

I looked at Charlie. "Notice anything about the ones we faced?"

Charlie thought for a minute. "A lot of them died from torn throats, I didn't see any defensive wounds, but then I wasn't looking for them, either."

I thought about my own kills. "That fits what I saw, too." I looked back over to Sarah. "What does that add to your theory?"

Sarah smiled. "A lot, actually. If I had to guess, I would say all of these people died the same night, and when they were sleeping. That accounts for the blood in the bedrooms. Next, we have something missing from this place, and something missing from the last town."

"What's that?" Duncan asked.

"Kids," Sarah said. "Where are the kids?"

I was speechless. In a sick way, it made sense. Zombie kids were different from the adults. The kids were faster, a lot more vicious, and in many cases, more intelligent that the average zombie. They were like the special forces of the zombie army.

I spoke up. "If you're right, then why would they leave? Why aren't they just hanging around like the adults?"

Rebecca shrugged. "Haven't figured that one out yet. But it's the only theory that fits the facts right now."

"All right," I said. "Let's get ourselves to the next town and see if it's the same. If it is, then at least we know what we're dealing with here."

As we climbed back into the vehicles, I looked over at Sarah and smiled. "Good thoughts."

"But?"

"A zombie kid army scares the shit out of me." Considering everything we had been through, it was as scary a thought as I had had in a long time.

CHAPTER 24

We drove east on Route 34, not having any real plan except to go to the next town on the list and see if there was anything to be learned. Given what we had so far, it wasn't very likely.

Sarah and I drove in relative silence, each of us lost in our own thoughts. Part of me thought we should have sent a message to Leport, but the other part asked what would we say. Everything we had up to this point was conjecture, and our operating theory was way the hell out there.

"Hey, John?"

"Yeah?"

"Why wouldn't a group of intelligent zombie kids make sense?"

"I guess I'm just being stubborn, since it flies in the face of everything we've seen so far. Maybe I just don't want to believe it," I said, looking over at her.

"Could be, but if you start with the dead coming back to life in the first place..." Sarah trailed off and I could see where she was going. We had seen the dead show signs of rudimentary group behavior, and several had shown limited problem solving abilities, including how to open doors and set up crude ambushes.

"You do have a point. I suppose it just scares me, since all the kid zombies we've seen so far have been nasty, quick little suckers, and if you throw some form of intelligence on them, then everything changes." I dodged a crack in the road and watched in the rearview as Charlie hit it head on. The van bounced and I laughed as I imagined the cursing going on in there right now.

"How far to Hastings?" I asked.

Sarah checked the map. "About twelve miles. Are we going to take a look at Malvern? That was on the map as being black, too."

I shook my head. "The first group to be sent out was weeks ago. They were just checking the first town to go dark. Likely, they found the same things we did, so they moved on. If I had to guess, they bought it at Malvern, which caused the second group to go out. We may find an answer or two at the third or fourth town, which is Hastings."

The countryside passed by slowly, and here and there, were some farms on the sides with their untended acres slowly reverting to pre-human status. Eventually all of this would be forest, and little to any sign humans had been here at all. Even the grass on the side of the roads was pushing its boundaries. It would be a long, long time before things got back to what we would consider normal.

Sarah saw the camp before I did. "Look over there!" She cried, hitting me on the arm and causing me to swerve slightly.

I slowed down and came to stop. A quick check of the map told me where I was and what I was looking at. Outside of Hastings was a decent sized river, and the river oxbowed at this point east of the town. The water was wide and deep enough to form an effective barrier, and the surrounded land had only a half-mile space between riverbanks. Inside the protected area was nothing but forest, creating a very defendable place. It made sense, then, to see three vehicles parked quietly across the river in a small clearing close to the water.

"Let's go check it out," I said, moving ahead and crossing the next bridge. I drove into the grass and made my way slowly across the fields and around the water. In the past, this area had been farmed, and the farmer had driven over the same area hundreds of times, creating nearly a road to where I needed to go. I thought it was convenient as hell.

When I reached the edge of the trees, I parked the truck, and the van parked behind me. Jumping out, I grabbed my carbine from the truck, letting everyone know it was time to go to work.

"Saw the vehicles, did you?" Tommy asked, flicking the safety off his rifle.

"Yeah. You, Charlie, and Rebecca take the far side, I'll take this side with Duncan and Sarah, and we'll meet on the inside by the trucks. Charlie, what's up?"

Charlie was squatting over by the grass, looking intently at something on the ground. Pulling his knife, he stabbed whatever it was and picked it up, inspecting it closely.

Stepping over to him, I saw what it was and sighed. "Great. Here we go."

Sarah looked over and shook her head, and Duncan peered around and got an eyeful when Charlie stuck it out to show everyone.

"Yuck," said Tommy as the severed finger was displayed. It didn't even look like a clean bite. It looked more as if the finger had been bitten and then torn off.

Charlie pointed to the spot where he had been standing. "Something strange out there. I can see several spots where something sat and bent the grass down, like it had been there for a few hours. Then the trail leads away from the camp. Over there," Charlie pointed to the south, near the river, "is the same thing, only the trail leads into the camp."

"Odd. You think it was living?" I asked.

"Explain the finger," Tommy said.

"Good point." We hadn't degenerated as a species yet to resort to cannibalism, although I hadn't visited the West Coast yet. Who knew what lay beyond the mountains? "All right, same plan. Keep your eyes open, and see if there are any other clues around here."

We split up and moved cautiously through the brush. The woods were heavy, but only about a quarter of a mile deep, so we could see fairly well. I thought I detected movement in the darker recesses, but since I wasn't chasing after it, I figured it would come to me.

We crossed a small section of brush and walked out in the open. This part of the peninsula had been mowed at one point, giving us tall grass, but no trees, and a gentle slope to the river. I could see the vehicles about six hundred feet ahead of us, so we would get there quickly.

That was the thought, until three zombies stood up out of the grass, and started working their way over to us. I didn't waste time with single combat. I fired a round into two of them, dropping them cold, while a shot from beside me took out the third.

"Nice shot, babe."

"Thanks, hon."

"No sharing, huh?" Duncan asked, miffed.

A snapping twig cut off my reply, so I just pointed to the two that came walking out of the trees.

"Cool. Thanks!" Said Duncan as he brought up his rifle. Three shots later and the Z count rose to five.

As we walked up to the nearest zombies, Sarah looked down, and then put her hand over her mouth. "Oh, no."

CHAPTER 25

I looked carefully at the torn face and lacerated throat, and realized I recognized the zombie on the ground. It was Jane Coswell, the leader of one of the groups sent out by Dot.

"Damn. All right, keep your eyes open. Chances are there's more," I said.

No sooner had I spoken those words than rifle shots sounded on the far side of the woods. First two shots, then a third. My guess was three more zombies just bit the dust.

We found the vehicles and looked them over very carefully. Four tents were on the ground, and one was still occupied. That poor soul was stuck in his sleeping bag, and glared at us impotently as Sarah shot him between the eyes.

Charlie and the rest came walking around the edge of the water, and immediately began looking through the other trucks. When he reached where I was, he raised an eyebrow in question.

"Six with the one in the tent," I said.

"Got three on the other side," Charlie confirmed.

"This is one of the groups sent by Dot," I added.

Charlie looked around. "How can you be sure?"

"Jane Coswell's over there. It's not good."

"Damn. She was a fighter."

"Any others you could see over on your side?" I asked, doing the math.

Charlie shook his head. "No, that was...wait. There's another. Tommy! South! By the trees!"

Tommy, who was closest, dropped the pack he was inspecting and stood quickly, bringing up his rifle. One shot later and the zombie who was sneaking up on the rear fell to the ground.

"That makes ten from here," I said. "We're missing one."

Charlie looked around. "Could be they're still in the bushes."

"Could be they ran." I pointed to the far side of the river where dried mud and matted grass came out of the water. The trail led up to the road and disappeared.

"Smart move. Where do you think they went?"

"No idea, but let's get this stuff out of here," I said. "We're running out of daylight, and I have no desire to stay here tonight."

"I heard that," said Tommy and Duncan in unison.

We drove the vehicles to the road and took everything we could use out of them. The team that had perished was well provisioned, and we stocked up on a lot of ammo. We took the time to say a small prayer for our comrades, expressing the regret that they had not been able to see the Upheaval to the very end. The empty trucks were a stark reminder to us that whatever was out here, it was extremely dangerous, and we could not take anything for granted.

We drove into Hastings as the sun was starting its final quarter descent. A fall wind was picking up, stirring the long grasses and saplings along the sides of the roads. A quick right turn and a half-mile later took us to the outskirts of Hastings. It was a small town, barely a mile square. The buildings were run down and abandoned, and the homes were slightly worse. If I had to make a guess, things were bad before the Upheaval.

We were moving down Indian Avenue, through the center of town when the radio suddenly came to life.

"Something's here. I just saw movement," Charlie said.

Sarah picked up the radio. "What kind?"

"Small and fast."

Sarah looked over at me. "Animal?" She asked.

"Negative."

"Copy that." Sarah looked at me, and I nodded.

"Let's get a look at our enemy, shall we?" I said, pulling over and stopping the truck.

I climbed out, and again I shook my head at the willingness of anyone wanting to live here. However, small towns were popular, and this one was no different. Trouble was this one, according to the reports, was just getting started again when they went dark.

I walked over to Charlie and said, "Where'd you see movement?"

He took out a tomahawk and pointed with it down the street called Harris.

"That way. It darted out on the next street up, headed the same way we were."

"Tracking us?" I asked.

"God, I hope not."

Charlie was right. If they had gotten to the point where they were tracking us, and not attacking right away, we were in trouble. I didn't want to think about that jump in intelligence.

CHAPTER 26

We loaded up and started to walk, splitting into three groups and staying to the center of the streets. It was an old practice, and made the most amount of sense, given the unfamiliar terrain. The good news was small towns like this one were generally laid out in a grid pattern, so it was easy to keep your bearings and agree upon a rendezvous point. Sarah and Rebecca were together, and Tommy and Duncan were another group, while Charlie and I made the third. We had worked together like that for so long it would have been strange to suggest any other pairings.

Charlie and I took the route directly towards where he had seen the movement, so we might get a look at our sneaker. It was possibly a feral kid, one of the thousands of orphans we had found in our travels. Sometimes they willingly came with us, sometimes they didn't. Once or twice, we left them alone, figuring them too far gone ever to adjust to a community. A few times, we had to put them down, their minds completely reverting to an animal state of insanity, and were a danger to others.

The walk towards the next street was uneventful, and I noted the litter and debris in the ditches. Charlie saw it, too, and his expression mirrored my own feelings. People in this town stopped caring long before the end of the world.

At Platte Ave, we moved south, carefully checking the darkening corners and behind fences and porch railings. There were a lot of places to hide in a town, and we didn't have time to find them all. In fact, we had about an hour before I called it quits and we found a secure place for the night.

At Hale, we turned east, and it was more of the same. Homes with unkempt yards, dilapidated garages and rusting cars. I guess the people who wanted to settle here had a thing for projects and fixer-uppers. Speaking of people, we hadn't seen any people at all, living or otherwise. We'd have to do a house search once we found our little ghost.

"There!" Charlie whispered, bringing up his rifle. I covered the other side, in case there were surprises. We moved carefully down the street, keeping an eye on the shadows.

"He's not moving. He's just staring at me," Charlie said. He was looking through his scope, so he could clearly see his adversary.

"Living or dead?" I wanted to know so we could determine this threat.

"Living, it looks like. Wait. Nope, he's dead."

"Are you sure?"

"Oh, yeah. He moved back into the darker area and his eyes are glowing."

That would do it. "We're clear on this side, take him out..."

Suddenly, a burst of gunfire from the east shattered the quiet we were walking in, startling several birds into flight.

"Jesus!" Charlie cursed, and then he cursed again. "Son of bitch!"

"What? What happened?" I kept my rifle up, scanning for threats.

"Little shit disappeared." Charlie sounded disgusted.

"Hate to bring more bad news on you man, but that's really bad," I said.

Charlie kept his rifle at the ready, scanning the bushes and corners. "Why?" he asked.

"When was the last time a little zombie had you in his sights and didn't attack?"

"Oh, hell."

"Yeah, let's find out what the others are shooting at. Maybe they got lucky." I walked away and Charlie held back, adjusting the sling on his rifle. I was about fifty feet away when I turned back and meant to say, 'You coming?'

Only what I said was, "Charlie, behind you!" I couldn't shoot. I could only watch helpless as a little zombie boy, running like a fiend from Hell, burst from his hiding place and raced for Charlie's unprotected back.

Had it been anyone else but Charlie, they would have died, myself included. Charlie dropped to one knee, pivoted around. In the same motion, he unslung a tomahawk and had it swinging just in time to smash it into the snarling, hissing face of the little Z. I had never seen Charlie move so fast in the entire time I had known him, and for a second I had to wonder if he hadn't been taking it easy on me all these years of practice.

I almost congratulated him, but I choked off the noise when a second zombie raced out of hiding, and launched itself at Charlie. Charlie was stuck trying to remove his 'hawk from the dead boy's head, unable to stop the little bastard. His hands shot forward to ward off the Z when suddenly she was hurled back, her head blasted apart by a .45 caliber bullet.

Charlie looked over at me and nodded. "Nice shot."

"Thanks. Good work on the first one," I said as I holstered my pistol.

"Thanks. Let's get the hell away from here, shall we?"

"My thoughts, exactly."

We jogged over to where we thought the shots had come from, and skidded to a halt as four rifles came up to zero in on us before we were recognized. Sarah and Rebecca came over to see the two of us, and Duncan and Tommy were looking over a pair of small forms on the ground.

"What have we got here? A couple blocks from here, we found two more." I said.

Duncan answered. "These little guys were hanging around this building, not sure why. We thought they were living until we got close enough, and Tommy saw they had been bitten on the arms."

Sure enough, they were both sporting matching bite marks in their upper arms. I found that to be odd, but this whole situation was turning into one big WTF moment.

"Wonder why they were hanging around here?" Sarah asked.

In answer, a door to the building, which was the town hall and community center, slowly opened. Charlie and I stood in front of it, but the rest of the crew spread out to have clear fields of fire.

Out into the open came a very thin figure, looking extremely haggard, yet very much alive. He still wore his weapons, but he looked like he hadn't slept in a while, and his last meal was a distant memory. His eyes were clear, which helped, and they locked right onto mine.

CHAPTER 27

"John Talon, I presume?" said the man, stumbling over and standing by the little corpses. He looked down and shook his head. "Hope you got the other two."

It took me a minute to recognize the man, given his appearance, but it was still a shock. "I'll be damned. Richard Loftuss. What the hell is going on out here?"

Richard shook his head. "Those little fuckers had me bottled up in that building for the last week. I managed to kill three of them, but the rest stayed out of sight, and I didn't have the ammo to hunt the rest of them. They wouldn't let me sleep, banging on the doors all night long, and I had no shot at them when they did." Richard took a deep breath. "Anyone else make it away from the camp?"

Charlie shook his head. "We killed everyone over there, they had all turned."

Richard hung his head for a minute, and then looked up at me. "You can't blame me for running. They were tearing us apart before I knew what was happening. I had gone to the riverside to piss, and suddenly the place exploded. Screams and shots, and glowing eyes running everywhere." He shook himself, and took a step back. "I fell into the river and made for the other side, hoping I could at least open up on the bastards from the riverbank. By the time I got to the other side, it was all over. I ran like hell for the town, figuring to rally the people here and make a stand."

Duncan spoke up. "What happened to this town?"

Richard shook his head. "They were gone when I got here. No idea where anyone was. I got chased all the way from the river, and by luck found this place open. Most of the horde moved on, those four stayed to get me."

"I was about at the end of things when I heard your shots and figured... Aaahhhh!!!"

Richard screamed as one of the little corpses suddenly lunged and locked its teeth onto his ankle, tearing at the flesh and spilling blood onto the street. Richard fell back, rolling away from the zombie, while Tommy fired from the hip, hitting the zombie in the head and killing it for good.

"God damn it!" Richard yelled over and over. "Son of a bitch!" he gripped his ankle, and blood dripped through his fingers.

I looked over at Duncan, who looked ashen.

"I shot it in the head! I know I did!" Duncan said.

"Let it go. Happens sometimes," I said. I went over to Richard and squatted down by him. He was gripping his ankle and gritting his teeth. He had calmed down, somewhat.

"Go figure. Hold them off until rescued, then they play dead until someone gets close." He was breathing heavy, and I knew what was coming.

"Sorry, Richard. Can you tell us anything about what we're dealing with here?" I asked.

Richard smiled sickly and shook his head. "Your man's screw-up killed me. Go to hell." He suddenly pulled his gun and pointed it at Duncan. Charlie's bullet took Richard in the head and he fell back, his life spilling out of a new hole in his head.

I stood up and looked over at my crew. Duncan was shaking his head, Charlie was frowning, Rebecca and Sarah were looking worried, and Tommy was poking the other zombie with his rifle.

"Well, we actually have a few more answers than we did, and we know what we're dealing with for sure. We've got to find some place to hole up for the night, if these things are in the area," I said.

Duncan spoke up. "John, I'm..."

I cut him off. "Don't apologize. He should have known better. For all his help, he should have stayed at his camp and died there." I was angry at Richard's selfishness, and angry at the situation. "We need to find a place to spend the night, and we need to talk, but this isn't the place."

I walked away from the scene and Sarah stepped in beside me, with Charlie and Rebecca behind us, and Tommy following. Duncan brought up the rear, after taking another long look at the mess on the ground.

We piled into the vehicles and drove away from Hastings, leaving behind Richard Loftuss and his killers. The sun was nearly down, and I wanted to find a place to spend the night safely. I didn't know where the band of little zombies was, and I wanted to make sure we weren't on a collision course.

Sarah wanted to talk when we got into the vehicles, but I shook my head. I was realizing we had made one right move and several wrong ones, but since we knew what we were now dealing with, we had to make the right moves, and we needed to do it as a group.

CHAPTER 28

I drove on Route 34 for about fifteen miles until I found what I was looking for. On the south side of the road was a grain elevator complex, and four huge silos were standing like silent sentries over the plains of Iowa. We were just north of Red Oak and Red Oak's airport, but I wasn't interested in the town this evening. I had no idea if Red Oak was alive at all, and I wasn't going to go exploring in the night. We had about twenty minutes left of daylight and we still had a lot to do.

I pulled the truck into the complex and around to the silos. I drove the truck right into the middle of the four towers, having barely enough room to pass through the south two of them and parked, giving Charlie enough space to park alongside me. The two vehicles took up most of the space in the courtyard of the silos. Above us, grain chutes crossed each other from tower to tower, forming a large X above our heads. To the north, we could see the road we had just left. To the west were just fields, and to the east and south were the maintenance buildings and control centers. A brick tower on the south reached up to the night sky, nearly as tall as the silos themselves.

As I got out of the truck, Sarah made a comment about feeling as if she was at the bottom of a well, but Charlie nodded approvingly at my choice.

"Good control of access points. Four bottlenecks that we could hold for a long time. Nice one," he said.

I shrugged. "When in Iowa..." I motioned for everyone to gather around, and I spread a map onto the bed of the truck. It was the one with the black circles. "Here's where we are," I said, pointing to a spot outside of Red Oak. Red Oak was one of the black circles, and it was a concern, because it was one of the larger cities in the area. "We have to figure that the band of little zombies has been through this area and are fast moving east. Chances are they aren't after anything specific. They are just building their army with more and more little ones. That would explain why the only ones left in the last towns were adults." There were murmurs at this, but I pressed on. "What I think our best course of action right now is to get ahead of them, warn the towns to re-fortify against the threat, and maybe get a chance to strike at these things."

I put away the map and Charlie and Sarah nodded. Tommy had that look on his face and Rebecca was thoughtful as well. Duncan was the first to break the silence.

"What I don't get," Duncan began, "is how these little bastards came into being in the first place? It flies in the face of everything we know about the zombies."

Before I could answer, Rebecca spoke up. "Actually, it doesn't," she said. "We've known for a long time that the virus took out the host and reanimated the body. One of the things we've also known is the older the host at the time of infection, the slower and more limited it was. The younger the host, the faster and more capable."

We all nodded and waited for her to go on. We were familiar with this stuff, Rebecca continued. "The thing we didn't realize was the body resisted in layers when it came to the brain. Typically, the brain will shut down non-functioning systems in an effort to save itself. This isn't new. However, what happened was the layers were responsible for different aspects of a person's development. The deeper the destruction, the less capable the zombie. What I think happened with these zombies, and is happening with the ones they are infecting, is the layers aren't being completely stripped away, and what's left is infected, but relatively intact."

I had to speak up. "Okay, you lost me in the layers, there. What are you saying?" Charlie nodded in agreement. Apparently, he was lost, too.

Rebecca smiled. "Okay, think of a brain as being capable of certain things based on size. A lizard is capable of limited functions, no learning capability, and no emotion. A cat has limited functions based in instinct, limited learning capability, and limited emotion. A dog has increased functions, superior learning capability, and the ability to feel true emotions. What I think happened with these zombies is they have had much of their brains wiped out, but a good portion remained, albeit infected. They are probably as smart as cats, but unable to feel any emotion. They are exhibiting pack behavior, and probably have a leader."

We all let that sink in. It fit with everything we had seen so far, and possibly gave us a chance to predict future behavior. It seriously changed the rules of engagement, and we would have to hunt them, while being hunted ourselves.

Duncan suddenly spoke up. "The school!"

Sarah looked over. "Explain."

Duncan smiled. "Remember the school in Glenwood that looked like it had been occupied, but a door was open? Anyone want to bet that's where our little band of marauders came from there?"

Duncan had a point. During the Upheaval, a lot of schools had been used as safe points for keeping kids out of harm's way. It wasn't inconceivable that a group had been holed up at a school, got infected, turned, and eventually figured out how to get out of the school.

"No bet. My guess is we need to skip these towns here, move as fast as we can to find an uninfected town, and start the warning process. Then we can alert the army and get them out here. The only thing we have going for us at this point is we're able to move faster and we have the river to keep them from Illinois."

We broke apart and went to our various places to rest. Sarah and I stayed in the truck while Duncan and Tommy slept in the van. Charlie and Rebecca went up to the tower across the way, with the notion of being in a high spot in case of attack.

CHAPTER 29

In the morning, we got back on the road and moved into the town of Red Oak. Red Oak was a big town with a decent sized population. The upside was it had weathered the Upheaval pretty decently, and a lot of people from surrounding areas had come here for protection and to escape the isolation of the farm country. Instead of a fence or border, they had gone the route of everyone being responsible for protection, and had built observation towers around the town to warn of any dangers. They relied on communication and everyone doing their part. You couldn't live there if you didn't want to contribute or participate.

As we approached the town proper, a man standing by a tower on the side of the road hailed us. The tower was a mixed-build affair, with concrete walls reaching ten feet up, made higher by a wooden structure that extended another fifteen feet in the air. A small, solid shack that had a little water tower, a stove, and several antennas topped it. I had been in one of the towers a few years back and it was a cozy little place. I stopped the truck alongside the man. I recognized him from the earlier years, and he hadn't changed much, just a little grayer on top and a little more wrinkled around the eyes.

"How do? You all just passin' through? Holy Shoot! John Talon! Sarah! Git out here!" The man stepped back and the two of us got out shaking hands and giving hugs.

"How you been, Jason? Good to see you're still kicking."

"Can't complain, can't complain. Who's in the other van?" Jason squinted and suddenly turned serious. "Is that Charlie? Who else you got in there? Duncan and Tommy?"

I nodded and Jason gave me a look. "You here about the outbreak?" He asked.

"What outbreak?" I decided to see if Jason would confirm our theories.

"We've had an outbreak on the south end of town, can't explain what the hell happened. People went to bed just fine, and then the next day they're attacking their neighbors. We've been under a lot of stress just keeping it under control. We've been sweeping daily for a couple of weeks, and we think we've gotten it handled, but it's been tough. The last couple of days have been quiet, so we think we may have it covered," Jason said.

"Did you call anyone about it? Maybe get some help?" I asked, wondering if the third team had been here.

Jason shook his head. "Our equipment got blown up when a zombie caught fire and walked into the generator gas supply. The radio was next door. Now that you mention it, a team did show up from the capitol, but they didn't stick around."

Jason looked at me hard. "What's going on, John? This is my home now, and if there's something happening related to these outbreaks, we should know."

Jason was right and I quickly outlined what we knew and suspected. He listened, and his eyes got wide at the description of the attackers, especially at their behavior.

"Dang. Well, you got work to do, so I won't keep you from it. Thanks for the heads up, and we'll keep our eyes open." He went back to his tower and threw a wave to Charlie and Rebecca as they drove past. I figured this town was going to be okay, unless the little devils came back. The part that was eluding me was how they were traveling from town to town. I couldn't find the connection.

We drove fast to the next town, but since the road wasn't the greatest, we took longer than I was hoping for. What should have been a twenty-minute drive actually took nearly an hour.

I pulled down the road to Stanton, and drove up to a water tower. As we got out to stretch, I had Charlie drive over to the tower and Duncan managed to get the ladder from the roof of the van. He quickly scampered up and he was gone for about ten minutes. When he came down, he had familiar news.

"Town's gone. Looks as if a last stand was made at the school, but there's nothing but corpses around here," Duncan said.

"Any good news?" Charlie asked.

"If I had to guess, the attack came from the south again, but I can't be sure. There's a good number of little dead zombies, so they made a good fight of it."

"Survivors?" I asked, already knowing the answer.

"Nope. I did see what looked like the remains of some heavy vehicles, so I'd say this was the last stand of the last team out here."

I did some mental math, and figured we were probably a week and change behind the last team out here. With the fight here, we were probably four days behind our little marauders.

Four days, and we were about two hundred and fifty miles from the border.

We were way too close to being out of time.

CHAPTER 30

At the junction of 34 and 71, I turned south to check out the town of Villisca. It was the only town in the area of any size, and with the way things were going; we couldn't just drive away from it. Sarah had rightly pointed out that, if it was untouched, they deserved to know what was headed their way. If we found several towns unharmed, we could at least know we had somehow gotten ahead of the threat and could prepare to meet it.

Villisca was only five miles away and the roads were actually pretty good, given the winters in Iowa, so we made decent time. At West High Street, we turned into the town proper and it was easy to see it was still alive. There was a lot of activity, and a lot of people moving around. A kid on a bike rode up to us, and gave us directions to the High School, where efforts were being coordinated to deal with the current outbreak.

We found the high school and a small, round, and heavily tattooed woman came out to meet me. She was about five feet tall, five feet wide, with bright red hair and a cigar hanging out of her mouth.

"Who the hell are you?" She demanded, placing a hand on her hip where a revolver sat in a worn holster. A bandolier of ammo ran over her shoulder and I could see several loops were empty.

I scanned the area quickly, and noticed a couple of men lounging nearby, well-armed and waiting for instruction. To the south and west, I could hear occasional shots and shouts.

"Name's John Talon, this here's Charlie James, Tommy Carter, Duncan Fries, and Rebecca and Sarah. Looks like you've got an outbreak on your hands," I said.

"Ain't you brilliant? Yes, dummy, we've got an outbreak." She paused to listen to her radio, which had an ear bud in her left ear. "Cliff! Jenkins! They need help down by the bar and grill! Git movin'!" She turned back to me. "Heard of you. First president after the Upheaval. Nice to meet you. Heard about Denver, too. You and that Mr. James ought to be ashamed of yourselves."

Charlie had the decency to look away before he laughed, but I just let it go. I liked this woman, and I had no idea who she was.

Out of the corner of my eye, I saw Sarah straighten a little. "And what's your name, sweetie?" She asked, staring at the presumed leader of the town. Sarah didn't like anyone who was rude, especially to me. I guess I should be flattered, but I swear I got into more fights over it.

The leader turned her little black eyes on Sarah and stared back. "My name's Crystal, and you'd better watch that 'sweetie' bullshit, missy."

Sarah stepped forward and would have started a serious argument, but I put up a hand. "Enough. If you need help, ask. If not, don't be rude, we'll be on our way."

Crystal put both hands on her hips and started a 'Who do you think you are?' tirade that lasted a full minute. I let her run out of steam before I decided to end the conversation.

I stepped close and looked down at her, letting her know I now wasn't in the mood for nonsense. "Now, you listen for a change, because you have a question to answer...'Will I run your ass out of this town as a rogue threat to the country?' Before you think to answer that, yes, I have that authority, and yes, my crew here is fully capable of taking care of any objections you or your men might have. If we leave you here in charge it is because I allow it." I paused for a breath and Crystal looked shocked.

"I don't want to deal with this. I have bigger problems on my mind right now, and frankly, so do you. Answer my questions and we'll be on our way if you don't want our help."

Crystal was much more subdued, and answered my questions honestly, even if a bit sulkily. It seemed they had things in hand here. Since it was a recent outbreak, it took a few people by surprise, but they were getting it under control and were doing okay. I was glad to hear that, because I didn't want to spend time in a place I wasn't needed. When I asked about communications, she gave me a noncommittal grunt.

"We never had any. All we ever did was to send someone over to Stanton when we wanted to talk or get any messages," she said.

Well, that fit. "What's the nearest town to here, going east?" I asked as I climbed back in the truck.

"Nodaway, about four miles up County Road 54."

"Thanks. Good luck."

"Would you have run me out?" Crystal asked as I started the vehicle.

I looked at her for few seconds. "Not really. I'd have just shot you."

CHAPTER 31

County Highway 54 was little more than a two-lane road, with gravel driveways leading off in the distance to farmhouses and silos. There were spots of trees here and there, and I knew enough about farmland to know that was typically, where the creeks and waterways were. There were ponds scattered about, and the remnants of crops long forgotten and gone to seed. I saw there were still some patches of corn, but they went to feed the crows and critters that roamed freely over the land now.

The road took a sharp turn to the north, and before I knew it, I was riding up on Nodaway. The town was seriously in the middle of nowhere, and as we drove along the western edge, I could see that it wasn't much, even in its heyday. Several homes looked like they were in some dire need of paint, and it was old enough to show that it was like that even before the end of the world. Many homes were small, four or five room affairs, but they were sitting on three-acre lots littered with outbuildings, children's toys, and rusted out cars.

Sarah looked at me and shrugged, and I had to return the gesture. We hadn't seen anyone, alive or dead in this burg, and it was a little creepy. The roadmap said there was a population of one hundred and thirty two, but none of them was out and about.

I started to get that old familiar feeling when something was seriously wrong, and I was feeling it now about Nordaway. I called Charlie on the radio to see what he thought.

"Charlie?" I winced, as we went over some seriously nasty railroad tracks.

"Ouch. What's up?" Came the strained reply.

"What's your take on this place? Over."

"We're being watched. Over."

That was the feeling. I looked over at Sarah and she nodded, pulling out her handgun and checking the magazine at the same time. There was something wrong about this place, and I wasn't going to give it a chance to nail us. One thing I had learned over the years was to trust my instincts and this place was telling me to get the hell out now.

"All right. Let's pull out of here. If there is anyone here, they're holed up pretty well, and if they're dead, they're not going anywhere." I told Sarah to make a note of the place for the army when they came back to sweep this area.

"John." Charlie's voice came through again.

"What's up?"

"Duncan says he heard something funny when he stuck his head out the window."

"What is he, a dog? Talk to me, what about it?"

"He says to stop the truck, and roll the windows down."

"All right, just a minute." I rolled to a stop on the road just north of Tenth Avenue. There was a house off to the east and a grain elevator further down the road, its grey tubes reaching for the noon sky.

I opened the window and listened intently, marveling again how quiet the world had become since the Upheaval. I could hear some insects in the grass, and a small rustling of the corn stalks as the breeze played around the leaves, but nothing seemed out of the ordinary. Just as a started to pick up the radio to tell Duncan he was an idiot, I heard a sound that didn't belong there. I looked over at Sarah and she confirmed what I had heard.

"What the hell is that sound, and why is it familiar?" She asked.

"Don't know, but you're right, it is familiar." The sound died down, was quiet for a minute, and then it started up again. It was a weird clicking noise, as if someone was tapping two small stones together. Only there was a lot of the clicking, as if fifty people were clicking the stones together. It started, stopped and started again.

I opened the door to the truck and Sarah nearly had a heart attack.

"What are you doing?" She hissed. "You don't know what's out there!"

I waved her off as I stepped away from the truck. The door was still open and I wasn't planning on going any further than a few feet, but I wanted to find out if there was anything to see.

Looking over at Charlie and Rebecca in the van, I could see Charlie mouth 'What the hell?' at me, but I didn't think I was in any real danger, not yet anyway.

As I stood there, the clicking noise started again and this time it didn't let up. It seemed to be coming from the fields, so my first thought was it was insects. I had seen some serious grasshoppers out here on the plains, so that wasn't outside the possible when it came to the noise.

The sun was warm on my face and I took a step towards the field, picking up a stone in the road. I threw the stone far out into the field, and the clicking stopped immediately.

I got back into the truck and Sarah glared at me. I shook my head at her and said, "I think the noise was some of those big grasshoppers. They stopped when I threw the rock into the field."

Sarah relaxed then laughed. "Bugs. Jesus, we're jumpy. Better let Charlie know."

I agreed and got him up on the radio as we pulled away from Nordaway. Everything would have been normal except he had to ask a nagging question.

"So where are all the people then? Crystal said Nordaway was populated and we haven't seen anyone at all."

Well, that killed the relief. Suddenly, I was back on alert and looking very hard at windows and buildings, trying to get a sense of what might have happened to the people here.

I radioed back to Charlie. "Maybe we need to get up high again."

"Agreed. Find a tower and we'll send Duncan up again."

I laughed as I heard Duncan protest over the radio. "Got it. I want to get to 34 again and get off these lousy farm roads."

"Well, what's keeping you?"

"Talon out." I tossed the radio onto the seat while Sarah giggled.

CHAPTER 32

We moved north and the sun began its descent into the afternoon. The landscape was green turning to brown, and the winds occasionally brought a hint of the winter to come. Since the Upheaval, the winters had alternated from severe to not bad, with one being downright mild. That had been a bad year, since the zombies had been active the entire time and didn't give us a break at all.

A few miles up the road, we passed a farmhouse that was situated up on a hill. The owner had dug the ditches around his home deeper and cut a trench across his driveway. A drawbridge had been created with some big planks of wood, and that served as a workable gate blocking the driveway against anyone making it across the trench. As we passed and turned onto 34, the owner came out of his house to wave. We stopped for a moment and gave him the rundown of recent events and the seeming abandonment of Nordaway. He thanked us and we were on our way, but in the rearview, I could see the man checking his fortress for weak spots. I hoped he'd be okay.

A few miles up the road, we found a cell tower on the intersection of Ginkgo Ave and Route 34. According to the map, the town of Brooks was about a quarter mile from us, but I wanted to look around before I committed to anything. Charlie drove the van over to the tower and Duncan climbed up with a big pair of binoculars hanging from his neck. He got to the top in good order and radioed down.

"Looks like there's another grain elevator to the south of us, just east of the town of Brooks. There isn't any activity I can see from here, just some live activity on farms to the north," Duncan said.

Good enough. "All right. Let's go have a look at Brooks, and we'll set ourselves up for the night somewhere around here," I said.

We moved down into the town of Brooks and I was actually surprised to see it was dead. It was far enough off the beaten path that it wasn't a likely haven for anyone running from the cities, but then Sarah pointed out that the city of Corning wasn't far away, and a zombie could have easily made the trip once the Upheaval had taken full effect.

We drove into the town and saw a lot of old activity. Several of the homes showed signs of break-ins. There were old bones bleaching in the sun, and a house even had a truck rammed into the front. It was a common theme revisited once again in the annals of the Zombie War.

I stopped the truck on Commercial Street and got out, figuring to look over the maps again to figure out our next move. That was the plan, anyway. Funny thing about plans is that the second you work one out, if you listen hard enough, you can almost hear God laughing at you.

Tommy and Duncan spilled out of the van, and Charlie came over to my side. Rebecca and Sarah decided to find some relief in the tree-lined homes to the south of us, figuring to do a quick once over for supplies and trade goods.

"What's the plan, boss?" Charlie asked.

I pointed to the town of Corning. "This is a big place, and I remember it still being alive in the southern portions. If anyone is still there, and they haven't had any outbreaks, then we can safely say we've managed to get ahead of the threat and we can radio into the capital what we have."

Charlie nodded. "We've been gone for only two days, so we're actually doing pretty well, all things considered."

I was about to answer when the radio popped to life.

"John? Charlie?" It as Tommy.

"Go ahead."

"Better get up here." Tommy was fairly calm, but he sounded agitated.

"Where are you?" I looked around and all I could see was Sarah and Rebecca coming back to the vehicles with a small sack over Rebecca's shoulder.

"At the end of Commercial on the east side, right where it turns north."

"All right, we're on our way." I hooked the radio on my belt and pulled my rifle from the truck bed. Charlie trotted back to the van and grabbed his weapons. Sarah and Rebecca tossed their loot into the truck and geared up as well.

As a group, we walked down Commercial, noting the emptiness of the town and the destruction of long ago. Out of a house on the right, a Z came stumbling out of the ruins of his home, his dark grey skin and skeletal features marking him as one of the old ones. He limped slowly towards us, his right arm outstretched and his mouth open, seeing a meal for the first time in years. His eyes were milky and he was missing his left foot, which made for awkward mobility.

"Got it," I said, crossing the street and picking up a length of fencing as I did. When I got close enough, I smashed the zombie on the head, just as he opened his rotting mouth to groan. The heavy board easily cracked his skull, sending him on to eternity. Behind him, a female bounced off the doorway as she stumbled out, her dress torn and weathered. Her arms were shredded skin, and her legs were torn as well. This one looked like she had fought hard against her attackers before succumbing.

I took the same board and finished her off the same way, burying the edge into her skull and driving her into the ground. She lay next to her husband and hopefully, they could finally rest in peace together.

I went back to the group and we continued walking, keeping an eye out for more zombies. Over the years, we discovered that quiet towns usually had zombies hiding out indoors, some bizarre survival instinct keeping them out of the detrimental effects of weather. It made a kind of sense, but it was creepy, too.

Two houses up and another zombie came out to greet us. This one was a teen that was missing its left cheek, exposing black teeth almost to the ear. Its nose was gone, leaving a black hole in the face, and one eye was gone as well.

Charlie stepped over to this one and when it reached for him, he kicked it in the chest, knocking it into an overgrown bush. The zombie struggled for a moment, but ceased when Charlie tapped it on the noggin with one of his tomahawks.

Right at the edge of the populated area, three more zombies came out for the party. Sarah stepped up to the smallest one and busted its skull with her spike. Rebecca stabbed a second one in the mouth with her spear, kicking the other one down as she did so. As it landed on the ground, Sarah was already stepping up to kill it. Charlie and I just watched in admiration.

CHAPTER 33

As we walked further, I could see Duncan and Tommy crouched down by some trees. We ducked ourselves, and made our way over to where they were. In front of them was a swath of trees, and I could see a small river winding its way through the countryside. To the south of us was a railroad bridge, but the tracks were lined with trees. I could see the river extending to the south, forming a decent barrier to attack from that direction.

Tommy and Duncan were waving us over and I could see they were a little agitated.

"What's up?" I whispered, getting in low by the pair.

"Take these and look to the north of those trees on the other side of the water," Duncan said.

I looked and winced. There was probably a hundred, to a hundred and fifty zombies milling about on the other side of the river. They didn't seem to be agitated. They were just in wander mode, hemmed in by the river and the trees.

I handed the binoculars back to Duncan. "Glad we didn't shoot those zombies we met on our way over here."

"No shit," Tommy said. "What do you want to do?"

I thought about it for a minute before deciding. "May as well finish them off. Want to guess where they came from?"

"Son of a bitch," Charlie said. "Did they look fresh?"

I looked again. "As a matter of fact, yes. Guess we know what happened to Nordaway." I turned to Rebecca and Sarah. "Want some rifle practice?"

In reply, the two women nodded and ducked back under cover to jog back to the vehicles. In ten minutes, they were back, each carrying a .22 rifle and a small box of ammunition. We had long ago discovered the high velocity stuff easily killed a zombie at fifty yards, as long as you hit it straight, so this was going to be pretty easy.

Sarah loaded up and moved to a clump of bushes directly in front of the mass of zombies. Rebecca moved slightly further down, and into a grove of trees. Both were going to shoot from concealed positions, which lessened the chances of the zombies swarming across the river. All we had to do was watch the show.

Sarah opened the ball by dropping five zombies fairly quickly. When she'd shot her magazine empty, Rebecca started firing from her position. The zombies were pretty agitated, but since they didn't have anything more than noise to go on, they weren't in attack mode. Rebecca finished her shooting and Sarah opened up again. It was almost boring.

Charlie bumped me out of my observations and pointed back towards the town. The road we had come out here on had four zombies walking our way, obviously attracted to the noise. I figured we could do our part, so I told Duncan and Tommy to wait while Charlie and I dealt with this. We crept under cover until we left the firing line, and moved back towards the road. The zombies were spaced pretty evenly apart, so I thought it would be a good time to show my improving skills with my tomahawk.

"All right, watch this," I said, limbering up my arm. "I'm going for that old man in the front." I watched the man move for a minute, mentally calculating his rate of speed and his relative distance away, which was about twenty yards. I figured on about three full rotations, so I waited until he was about fifteen yards away and let fly. The black weapon sailed through the air, past my target, and buried itself in the lower abdomen of the zombie behind it. The unintended target didn't even slow down or acknowledge the eighteen inches of black polymer sticking out of its crotch.

I didn't want to look at Charlie. I really didn't. I could hear him, and that was bad enough.

"Say anything, and I swear I'll knock your stupid ass out," I said, trying to be as diplomatic as possible.

"Wouldn't dream of it." Charlie snorted, barely containing himself. "Oh, Duncan!" Charlie called.

"You. Suck," I said, pulling out my pickaxe for the converging Zs.

"What's up? Whoop! Zombies. Got a cure for that," Duncan said as he pulled out his sword. "Hey, that one has a black...tomahawk...in...its...crotch." Duncan stared. "Hey, John? Isn't that your axe?"

"No," I said as I stepped up to the old man. He reached out for me and snarled, rolling his eyes up as I crushed his skull with my pick. I kicked a second in the hip, knocking it to the ground, and buried the point in the top of another's head. I stepped over to the one holding my axe for me and speared it through the eye with my knife, jerking out my 'hawk as it fell. Duncan decapitated the last one, and I had to say again that the sword impressed me more and more.

The shots died down from the river at the same time, and Sarah and Rebecca came over to see if they could help. When they saw they couldn't, they shouldered their weapons and we all took a stroll back into town to get to the vehicles. I had to clean off my weapons and the ladies wanted to clean their weapons as well.

I looked at the sky and figured we had about two hours of sunlight left. It was a good time to find a place to hole up for the night. I didn't want to stay in town. There were too many ghosts out there, and enough leftover ghouls to make the weary weep.

We finished cleanup and drove out of brooks, heading east to the big grain elevator on the railroad. I was looking for a decent place to camp, and I was well aware of the dangers of camping out here in these woods in this particular situation.

The grain elevator was a massive complex, with three huge bins on the south end by the tracks, a tall building attached to a six-pack of smaller silos, and a very huge maintenance facility to the east. We drove past the big silos, and under the observation platform. Several freight cars waited on the siding, their cargos patient for transport that would likely never arrive. I circled past the big buildings, and went to the north side. I was looking for some space, some place that could give me a kill zone should I need it.

On the far north side, a small road led off through the fields, and led to a large construction site that had been cleared, but not developed. I could see the rolling hills in front of me, and I watched, as the shadows grew longer in the evening. I parked the truck in the middle of the area and waited. Charlie pulled the van up alongside, facing the opposite direction. We were going to be sleeping in the vehicles, but that was nothing new. We just wanted to make sure we were in a place we knew was safe. There was nowhere to hide for fifty yards.

Sarah and I wandered over to the van and we spent a good hour going over the maps and plans for where we wanted to go next. I figured we should just follow 34, since that seemed to keep us in the middle of things, while Tommy and Duncan wanted to just head for home and let someone else handle the mess. Charlie voted with me, and Sarah and Rebecca did as well. I could understand the two men, since they had young families to take care of, but we needed to be able to do what we could out here as best as we could. Besides, we hadn't found any viable communication yet.

When the sun went down, we went back to our truck and settled in as best we could. I took the front seat and Sarah curled up on the back. It would have been nice to be able to sleep together, but we could still talk and this mission wasn't going to last forever.

"John?" Sarah's voice drifted over the seats.

"What's up?"

"Why aren't we running for home? We know what the threat is and its general direction, why not let the army handle it?"

I admitted she had a point, but there was a good reason and I let her know. "If we take off now, the little buggers could shift direction and we'd be running blind. Meanwhile, town after town falls to them, with the dead kids building on their own army. If we keep nearby, find some communication, then we can lead the army right to them and watch the show."

Sarah mulled that one over and I could almost hear her nod. "That makes the most sense so far. Why didn't you mention it before?"

"Truth is, I just thought of it."

There was a silence then Sarah spoke in an awed voice. "I'll be damned."

"What?"

"You really do make this shit up as you go along."

"Go to sleep."

CHAPTER 34

At about two in the morning, I woke up. I couldn't say why, I just did. I sat up very slowly, letting my eyes look around without moving my head. Sarah was sleeping on her side, snoring very softly in the back portion of the seat. The sunroof was cracked open about an inch and the doors were thankfully locked. The driver's side of the truck was close to the van, and as I sat there, wondering what it was that woke me up so completely, I heard a noise outside between the two vehicles.

It was so subtle, gentle almost, like a caress. But there was no mistaking the sound for the wind. It sounded like someone or something was running their hand along the truck as they slowly walked around it. From where I sat, I would be face to face with it in seconds if I didn't move.

I slid down onto the seat and removed my sidearm from the center console. After a quick moment of thought, I realized I didn't have a shot, since the bullet could strike the van and hurt someone inside. Add to the fact that I would have to shoot through the window, it didn't work out as a viable solution. The upside, I was safe. There was no way a zombie could get in here. My concern was there might be others, and a confrontation would bring them in a hurry.

As I lay there, I kept my eyes on the window, hoping for some sign of what was moving out there. I couldn't see over the seats, as I was lying down, so my vision was limited to the passenger side. All I could do was wait.

After ten seconds, the top of a head appeared at the window. It was a scruffy head of hair, tangled and matted. From what I could see, it could have been an orphan, come out to check if anything interesting was in the two vehicles that showed up out of nowhere. I closed my eyes so I could barely see, but keep anything from seeing the whites of my eyes as I looked around.

The head stopped and I could see it slowly rising, as if the person were getting on their tiptoes. I breathed as quietly as possible, knowing the slightest sound would draw attention. I could hear Sarah still snoring, but I hoped it wasn't audible through the windows. The sunroof was cracked slightly to give us some air, but that was only done on a high vehicle like our truck. We learned a long time ago that windows opened even slightly were like giving a key to the door to a zombie. They just grabbed and pulled the windows out.

As the head rose, I could see a faint glow, coming from under the forehead, and I knew immediately this was no live orphan. This was a dead one and its eyes were in full bioluminescent glow. The head stopped as the eyes cleared the base of the window and it took all of my willpower not to shoot the damn thing, as it was inches from me. I knew it couldn't see very well, as the windows were slightly tinted, and it was very dark outside, just a sliver of a moon to light the landscape. But none of this was much of a comfort if the zombie decided to make an issue of things and bring a horde of little zombies our way.

The eyes darted around for a few seconds, and I had a moment of panic when they stared down at me. I had to resist the urge to move and bring my weapon to bear, as well as resist the urge to avert my eyes.

As slowly as they had risen, the head and eyes descended, and started to move to the front of the vehicle. I breathed a low sigh of relief and quietly eased myself to a semi-sitting position. I could see over the dash and hood, and saw the little zombie walking slowly away, its little hand running over the hood of the truck. I was actually in a bit of a dilemma, as I watched it walk around the front of the truck. Do I kill it now? Or do I let it go, note the direction it took, and hope it's part of the larger horde?

As I was contemplating this, the decision was made for me. The passenger side door was suddenly opened on the van and I could hear someone getting out. The zombie heard it, too and walked quickly around the front of the truck and in between the vehicles. If I didn't do anything, someone was going to have a zombie on them without warning. I didn't dare fire a shot, because the bullet would go through the zombie, then through the van. If anyone got hit, even just wounded, they were dead, because the virus would likely transfer on the bullet.

I took the easy route. When the zombie passed the driver's side door, I opened it hard, trapping the zombie between the vehicles, waking up Sarah in the process.

"What...who?" she said sleepily.

"Nothing dear, just killing a zombie kid, go back to sleep." My words of comfort had the exact opposite effect as the zombie scrabbled and clawed at the door, grabbing my pants as it tried to free its head from entrapment. Sarah jumped up and quickly assessed the situation.

"Hang on, I got it." She rummaged a bit and produced my trench 'hawk, exiting the vehicle from the opposite side and circling around the front. One spiked head later and the zombie dropped to the ground.

"You okay?" Sarah asked, checking my leg.

"Fine, very awake, too." I stepped over the fallen Z and went to the front of the van, where I ran head-on into Charlie.

"What's going on? I stepped out to take a piss and heard a ruckus on your side," he said

"Killed a Z that was coming after you. She'd have been on you before you knew it."

Charlie looked over my shoulder and winced. "Yeah, it would be hard to battle a zombie with my dick in the wind."

I shrugged off that mental image and was about to say goodnight when the grass around our open area began that clicking sound again. Charlie and I looked around and again I had that feeling I knew what that sound was, I was just having a hard time trying to figure out what it was.

"Those bugs are persistent," Charlie said, hitching his pants a little.

Sarah came up behind us and said, "I can't help but think I know I've heard that sound before, and it wasn't bugs."

I had to agree. I did a quick rundown of the things we had learned about our enemy on this trip and was coming up short. Nothing we had seen was telling me this was anything else but big grasshoppers, but my instincts were screaming at me that it was something else.

I thought about the survivors of the previous expeditions, and I kept coming back to the one camp that had been attacked in the night. That thought led me to the man I had shot over in Illinois. He said some crazy stuff, like clicking and teeth. I often wondered what he had meant by that.

Suddenly it hit me, and I shouted aloud. "Teeth! Jesus!"

Sarah and Charlie looked at me like I was nuts, and I swear Charlie looked at my teeth.

"That's what that guy in Illinois was talking about. Teeth clicking together! That's what that sound is. Now I remember where I've heard it before. Remember the pit of zombie heads that was like a pond of piranhas?" I looked out over the grass and heard the clicking intensify.

Charlie and Sarah heard it as well, and just as they were about to comment, about twenty zombie kids burst from the grass, racing towards us.

CHAPTER 35

"Christ! Back in the trucks! Get moving!" I yelled pushing Sarah ahead of me into the truck. I glanced over my shoulder and saw that Charlie had made it to his vehicle just in time. In seconds, little zombies, their hands pounding on the windows and grasping at the mirrors, surrounded us.

I yelled into the radio. "Get driving, head south towards the tracks and the silos! Stay close!"

"Got it. Nasty little things, aren't they?" Rebecca replied. She was driving the van. The big vehicle pulled away, dragging a few of the little creatures with it, as they were pulled under the van.

I pulled away as well, pointing the truck towards the road and to relative safety. We were effectively trapped. Unless we could shake these little rats, and unless we had some serious highway to use, then we were going to have them dogging us for a while. The good news was we were relatively safe in our vehicles. The bad news was we couldn't get out without getting swamped and killed.

I pulled through the grain elevator main area, with the van right behind me. Behind us, the zombies were running full tilt, and a glance at the speedometer told me they were good for fifteen miles an hour. I pushed it to twenty and the zombies began to fall behind. I couldn't go much faster, since I had to go around some pretty big obstacles, but that was fast enough.

Sarah was busy next to me, setting out magazines and getting the rifles ready. I was about to turn the truck towards a building when the radio popped on.

"John! Check your six!" It was Charlie and his voice was tight.

I looked back and could see the van, but nothing else. "What the hell?" I said aloud.

"What?" asked Sarah, looking up from her work.

"They're gone!" I was incredulous. "They're really gone!"

"Who, Rebecca?" Sarah turned her head around and looked back. "They're right there, silly."

"Not them, the zombies."

Sarah looked again. "What the hell?"

"Exactly. I'm starting to see why those communities fell so easily." I pulled the truck into the silos by the tracks, and the van pulled alongside. Between the two of us, there was only enough room to open the doors on the driver side on the truck and the passenger side on the van. Tommy and Duncan jumped out of the van loaded for bear and I pointed them to the opposite sides of the silos. Charlie, Rebecca, Sarah and I stood in the bed of the truck, giving us a chance to talk and cover the other two.

Charlie started us off. "What the hell?"

I concurred. "No shit. I've never seen a zombie break off pursuit, especially when it could still see us. That's just wrong."

Rebecca shook her head. "It was wrong. We're fighting these guys as if we're still fighting the first years of the Upheaval. If these little guys have had the time for the virus to simmer for a while, then chances are it's evolved into something we aren't used to."

Sarah nodded. "We've seen zombies that were able to learn rudimentary behavior after a lot of trial and error, and retain enough memory of the action to be able to do it again under similar circumstances. In this case, they have spent years learning and learning, and now they're free, we're just trying to catch up."

I looked over at Charlie. "I guess we know who the thinkers are of this group."

Charlie shrugged. "I know, I married up."

"Let's get back to the basics. What do we do?" I asked. "I'm willing to admit these are the smartest zombies we've come across, but they are not the smartest humans ever and are still motivated by hunger and the need to survive. They can be tricked and they can be killed. We just need to make sure we do both."

Everyone agreed, and we hopped off the truck in time to see Duncan running back to us.

"They're coming! They aren't running, so they may not know where we are yet," he said, checking his weapons.

I looked over at Tommy and whistled softly. Tommy looked over and shook his head. Nothing on his side. I had a feeling, so I told Charlie, Sarah and Rebecca to go to the front with Duncan, and I was going to be in back with Tommy. Charlie looked at me funny, so I answered his question. "If these things are smart, then they might split up. If they do, we can offer a surprise from our rear."

Sarah winked at me and took off for Duncan's position, checking her mags as well. Charlie loosened his 'hawks and Rebecca switched on the red dot sight on her rifle. She hopped into the bed of the truck and was going to be our backup from above should the need arise.

CHAPTER 36

I went back towards Tommy and took up a position next to him. He was kneeling and had his rifle trained towards the side of the silo. Spare magazines were ready and waiting on his leg. I moved a little further to his right and settled down in the same fashion. From my viewpoint, I could see just a little further. In front of me was a long set of railroad tracks that stretched out into the night. Long grass swayed slightly and bits of small stone turned over when a small gust of wind blew in from the south, stirring the area.

"Should we provoke?" Tommy asked, very quietly out of the side of his mouth.

"No, they can't know where we are until we kill them."

"Wish we could sneak a peek around the corner."

"Me, too." The hardest part of a situation like this was waiting. Most of the time it worked and we killed the Zs. Sometimes it didn't and we had to go out and find the zombie again, sometimes surprising them as much as we were surprised.

I did know that once the ball opened up on the north side, that the zombies would be attracted to the noise, but if we left our rear unguarded, we could be wiped out in a hurry if they circled around.

Everything was silent for a few long minutes. The wind picked up a bit and rattled the roof of the silo, causing Tommy and myself to jump a little. We shook it off and waited some more.

After a few minutes, I could hear them. They were walking slowly down the long road, nearly marching in unison. I could hear the crunch of the gravel as dozens of small feet walked towards our position.

By Tommy's stiffening posture, I could tell he was hearing it, too. We brought our rifle stocks to our cheeks and put our aperture sights on the area just next to the silo. The second anything showed up, we were going to blast it to hell.

Suddenly, the crunching gravel stopped. I looked over at Tommy and he shrugged slightly. This kind of behavior was way past what we were used to and I couldn't help but feel we were really behind the learning curve.

My thoughts were interrupted by a sudden blast of gunfire to the north. I could hear Charlie's rifle barking and Sarah's as well. Duncan was holding off until he had a shot. Rebecca was probably nervous in her perch, but I knew she was steady.

The firing stopped and there was a pause. Tommy and I waited, and then I decided to see what was up. Slapping Tommy on the shoulder, I sprinted for the north and stopped by Charlie. I could see six or seven small bodies out on the parking lot and that was it.

"What's up, are we done?" I asked.

Duncan spoke up. "There was way more than that in that group. Don't know where they are." Duncan looked agitated, as if we would blame him for misreporting the number of ghouls.

"They have to be out there, and if there are more, they sure know where we are now," I said.

Charlie nodded. "Should we pull out?"

I shook my head. "No, let's see if they try it again. We're in a good spot and we can thin the herd if they charge."

As I walked back towards the vehicles, I threw a wink at Rebecca, and then sprinted as I heard Tommy yell.

"John! They're here!" His rifle punctuated his words as he fired at his targets.

I skidded to a stop next to him and didn't bother to kneel. I fired at a glowing spot that moved quickly towards me and knocked a little zombie dead. I fired again, trying to shoot after Tommy did. He dropped three and I killed another two, killing the second barely two feet from our position.

"Getting closer," Tommy said, dropping his magazine and replacing it with a fully loaded one. He took a few loose rounds out of his vest and refreshed the used mag.

"I know. I feel like we're battling living people," I said, aiming my rifle at a clump of grass across the tracks that looked like it was moving.

"That'd be easier, since we could just shoot those anywhere and put them down," Tommy said.

I reflected for a second. "After all these years, I doubt I could shoot anything anywhere but the head."

Tommy contemplated that one for a second. "You know, you might be right." He looked hard for a second. "You see anything out there?"

"You mean those glowing eyes about a hundred yards out?"

"Yup."

"Rebecca!" I called.

A quiet reply floated down to us. "I see him." A loud crack, and a dead Z later, there was a second reply. "Got him."

That must have been some sort of signal, because suddenly there was a rush. A dozen little zombies burst from the grass and launched themselves at us. I didn't waste time trying to line up every shot for a kill. I just wanted to slow them down some. By the firing going on next to me, Tommy was feeling the same.

"Dammit, they're fast!" He said, quickly switching out another magazine.

"No kidding. Got you, you little bastard!" I cracked another one in the head and his headlong rush tumbled him another five yards. A second zombie jumped over the still corpse and raced towards us. Tommy fired and put him down, and then a trio of little girls came racing around the corner. I couldn't fire, because Tommy was right in my way.

"Your left!" I called.

Tommy swung his rifle up and just emptied his magazine at them. The bullets halted their forward progress and pushed them back, two of them being struck in the head and falling for good. The third, a girl of maybe eleven years, slowly got back to her feet. Her right arm was useless, having been shattered at the elbow by a bullet. Two more bullets tore her face, and her skin hung in ragged chunks, where a bullet had gone through her mouth. She glared at Tommy, and snarled with what was left of her mouth. It wasn't a pretty sight.

Tommy looked at her for a minute and then shot her between the eyes, killing her on top of her friends. He looked down at the tracks in the gravel and whistled when he saw the footprints just four feet from his spot.

"Too close. Way too close," he said.

"We got them, maybe that's it," I said.

No sooner had the words left my mouth than Rebecca shouted to us.

"John! Tommy! Hurry!"

CHAPTER 37

We ran up to the north side, taking opposite sides of the truck and van, and saw Duncan, Charlie and Sarah fighting for their lives. Sarah was kicking over a small zombie, while stabbing another in the eye. Duncan was holding off three with his sword, and Charlie was holding one by the neck while killing another with his tomahawk. In the open space to the north, I could see ten more sprinting across the parking lot towards us.

I quickly raised my rifle to fire, killing three before the rest split off and ran to the sides of the silo. Tommy killed another two on his side.

"About time!" Sarah yelled, bracing for the charge of the one she had knocked down.

"Just in time, I'd say," I said, drawing my pistol and blowing a huge hole in the head of the zombie scrambling to get up. I fired again at one of the zombies Duncan was dealing with, dropping him from the side.

"My thanks!" Duncan yelled. He leaped forward, swinging hard. His sword connected with a small zombie, lopping her head off. Duncan brought the blade around for another swing, this time kneeling when he struck, adding power to his swing. The long blade sliced a zombie completely in half, including the arms. The body fell in four pieces, with the severed torso struggling to use arms that suddenly had been shortened by half.

Charlie threw the struggling corpse of the zombie he was holding against the silo. It landed in a heap, but sprang up faster than it had fallen. When Charlie turned to deal with it, it was already on him. He managed to fling it off again, but not before the little zombie managed to bite him on the arm.

Charlie roared in pain and anger, and brought out his second tomahawk. The zombie boy, probably no older than seven when he originally had died, scrambled up again and charged one last time. Charlie chopped him into little nasty chunks, saving the killing blow for last.

Sarah was the first one to notice Charlie had been bitten. She touched my arm and pointed to Charlie. I stopped scanning the grass for more threats, and then waved Rebecca down. Charlie was holding his arm, staring down at the reddening wound on his forearm.

We gathered around Charlie and Rebecca started crying. Sarah took her to the van and told her it was going to be okay. I looked at Charlie.

"Where do you want to do this?" There wasn't much else to say.

Charlie looked around. "That parking lot is as good a place as any."

"All right. Your call." I waved over to Tommy and Duncan. "Keep them off us, all right?"

Duncan looked down while Tommy answered. "Will do. I think they're gone, though."

I listened to the wind blowing, and thought I heard some clicking to the east, but chances were it was just stones.

Charlie and I walked over to the parking lot, and Charlie took the time to take off his weapons. His 'hawks, he placed gently on the ground, and then he removed his knife and pistol. Charlie then faced me and shook my hand one last time.

"Good luck," I said.

"Thanks. You'll be okay?"

"I will. You've been a good friend and brother."

"You too. See you on the other side."

Charlie lay down on the asphalt, his injured arm held away from his body. I stood watch, making sure we had no surprises when things came to their inevitable conclusion.

While I waited for Charlie, I looked around at the landscape. In the lean hours of the morning, I could just make out the dark shapes of the hills to the north. The setting moon provided just enough light to see, but not enough to be useful in finding targets.

After twenty minutes of lying still, Charlie began to twitch slightly. His arm spasmed and jumped a little and I knew it wasn't going to be too long, now. I checked my pockets to make sure I had what was needed, then waited some more. Sure enough, the heavier spasms hit, and Charlie's back arched briefly. His body clenched itself, with his arms and legs bending, bringing him to a fetal position.

Slowly, slowly, his body straightened out, and I could see his arm was very red, with black where the zombie had bitten him. I reflected on all the things we had been through, all of the fights we had survived without so much as a scratch. It always seemed to happen this way. I started to get angry at the whole situation. First, I was angry at Dot, then I was angry with the people sent out here, who couldn't handle the problem, then I was mad at the townspeople who had died, and finally I had just enough anger left for the little shit that had bitten Charlie.

After an hour of Charlie lying perfectly still, his hands began to move. After a minute, he rolled over onto his stomach and carefully put his hands by his head. Pushing up, he got his legs under himself and stood very slowly, bits of rock that had clung to his clothes falling to the ground. I placed a hand on my sidearm and waited.

Charlie brought his hand to his head and shook it slightly. He turned and spotted me standing there. Moving in my direction, one-step at a time, Charlie opened his mouth.

CHAPTER 38

"Ouch."

"No doubt. Aspirin?" I held out a small bottle of the pills and a canteen.

"Please. Jesus, I have a headache." Charlie shook out six of the pills and tossed them down his throat, chasing them with large gulps of water.

After a minute, he took a huge breath and gathered up his things. He put his gun and knife back, and replaced his 'hawks. Steadying himself, he opened his pack and pulled out a packet of penicillin. Crushing the pills, he scattered the powder over his wound, and wrapped it up with some gauze.

"How do I look?" Charlie asked.

I looked at him critically. "Your eyeballs are glowing."

"What?"

"Just kidding."

"That wasn't funny."

We walked slowly back to the vehicles and I could see the crew waiting in the vehicles. As soon as they could see us, Rebecca came racing out of the van and nearly toppled Charlie over. I swear her hug almost popped his head off.

Sarah came out to meet me and I gave her a hug and kiss as well.

"All good?" she asked, looking over at the other couple.

"Yeah, this one wasn't as bad as the last," I said. A long time ago, we had a doctor who decided, for whatever reason, to take blood samples of everyone who was living in the community. I thought it was for transfusions should the need arise, but the good doc had figured that anyone surviving the Upheaval, given how contagious the virus was, had to have some kind of immunity. As it turned out, Charlie was immune. I was informed that I was probably immune as well, but I had never tested it, and wasn't really willing to try. Charlie first got bitten in Nebraska, then a second time in Denver. Each time the virus tries to take over and each time Charlie manages to fight it back. Every once in a while he makes a trip to the capital to donate some blood for testing and an attempt at an anti-virus. So far, no luck. Charlie gets to suffer through some serious headaches, and his spasms once broke a window, which is why we moved to the outdoors when the bite in Denver occurred.

Charlie said the fight royally sucked, and his head felt like someone had shot him in the forehead, but other than the bitten area becoming little black teeth marks, he was none the worse for wear.

Rebecca redressed the wound and Charlie settled into one of the back captain's chairs in the van. Tommy was going to drive for a while.

I looked at the corpses surrounding us and then at the lightening sky. I decided we needed to rest a bit, so I climbed aboard the truck and we pulled out of town. I moved north until I hit 34, then pulled over onto the driveway of a small farm. Radioing back to the van, I said we needed to catch up on sleep, so we would stick around there for a few hours. Everyone agreed, so we slipped back into the sleep we left, after what seemed so long ago.

Sarah practically fell onto me and we dropped the seats back to rest. As I fell asleep, I swore I could hear clicking in the wind.

CHAPTER 39

"What's the link?"

"What?"

"Oh, sorry. Talking to myself. Did I wake you?"

"No, I was up."

I leaned over and kissed Sarah good morning, and then turned back to my map. I had a large Iowa map spread out over the steering wheel and I was staring at the marks we had made.

"I've been over this map, and over it, and I'm trying to figure out what is linking these communities together," I said, tracing a finger over the towns we'd marked and the ones we had been to, frustrating myself.

Sarah leaned over to look at what I was doing. "There aren't any clear roads that travel that way, and there's a river that the zombies would have to cross." She looked up. "Huh. That is curious. How are they able to get to these towns and then get away? Somebody should be able to track them, especially if there's as many as we think there are."

I put the map away and got out of the truck. The morning was giving way to noon, and the sun felt good on my face. The grasses around me whispered gently, and the breeze stirred leaves ready to start turning and falling.

I went over to the truck to see how Charlie was doing and ran into Rebecca.

"Whoop! Excuse me. Good morning. How's Charlie doing this fine day?"

Rebecca smiled. "I worry like hell, and the big doofus pulls through. His arm is infected from the bite, so we'll have to keep an eye on it, but I think he'll live."

I smiled. "Figures, even zombies can't kill that goof. Sarah's up, just so you know."

"Thanks."

I looked inside the van and Duncan was still sprawled across the floor on the other side. Tommy was up and stretching, and Charlie was sitting in a chair, flexing his hand and looking at his bandaged arm.

"How's the wing?" I said as a hello.

Charlie's face smiled a little. "Hurts, but I'll be fine. The headache is the thing, though. That sucker will knock you out. How's Sarah?"

"She's fine. We were going over the map today, trying to find the link between the towns, hoping to be able to get a line on where our little friends might strike next, but damned if I can figure it out," I said.

"What kind of link?" Tommy asked, thumping Duncan on the side to wake him. Duncan responded by turning over onto his other side and snoring into the base of the sidewall.

"I don't get how these things are making their attacks. They are not staying in one place, but they're not following any roads. They're crossing rivers and streams with ease, and nothing seems to slow them down. I'm actually afraid of where they might be today." I was concerned, since we were deep in Iowa, and I didn't want to chase my tail for another day.

Tommy looked thoughtful while Charlie answered. "Do we have a plan for today, anyway?"

I nodded. "I figure we'll just try to get ahead of them, make sure people are defended, and have some communication, and triangulate their position by their attacks. If people know what they're up against, they can prepare for it. "

"When are we moving?" Charlie asked, getting out of the chair and grabbing Duncan by the belt. Duncan let out a sleepy squawk as Charlie hauled him out of the van and dumped him out on the ground.

Duncan opened his eyes and looked up at me. "When's breakfast?"

"Lunch is on the road. Get ready, we're moving fast. You're on communication. I need you to get in touch with anyone out there. We need a starting point and I'm sick of being down ten points after the first quarter." I headed back to the truck and passed Rebecca on the way. She was smiling and I figured she had a right to be.

We moved out of our camp about twenty minutes later, munching on supplies as we followed Brooks road on its winding path towards 34. Once we reached 34, I headed east, and in a short amount of time, we reached the outskirts of Corning.

Corning was the county seat, so it was a little bigger than the other small towns. That was either a good thing or a bad thing. More people usually meant increased chances of infection, while at the same time, having more defenders was always a good thing.

Unfortunately, Corning had gone down in the Upheaval, and it didn't look like anyone had tried to make any attempt to relocate there. We slowed long enough to see that the place was abandoned and empty, and then we moved on. There might have been people on the other side, but I had to keep moving. I had a feeling the answer to my dilemma was right in front of my nose, but all I could see was brick walls.

Trying to make up for the rest that we took, I moved along 34 as best I could, and waited for any contact from Duncan from any towns. Prescott was quiet, as far as I could tell, so we moved towards Creston. Creston once boasted a population of over seven thousand, but it was limited to a little over five hundred these days. In the upheaval, the northern portion of the town was gone, but the southern section held their ground and managed to fight off the mess from the north. The southern Crestons were tough people, used to fighting and unafraid of zombies. We were lucky to have two hundred of them join us in our fight across the country.

Just before we reached the outskirts of Creston, Duncan radioed in.

"John! John! Talk to me! Over!"

Sarah grabbed the radio as I navigated around a particularly deep pothole.

"Sarah here, what is it?"

"Creston's in trouble! They're calling for help. Sounds like they've had an outbreak and it's a bad one!"

"Got it. Get ready. Over." Sarah looked at me and I just shook my head.

"Dammit. We shouldn't have rested," I said.

"Nonsense. Charlie was bitten and we were exhausted." Sarah tried to make me feel better, but I still felt like it was my fault. Seemed like every decision I was making this trip was leading to disaster.

"All right." I grabbed the radio. "Duncan, everyone. Gear up, we're going in fast and heavy." I pushed the truck a little faster, hoping we could make it in time.

CHAPTER 40

We rolled into the south end of Creston and raced along Taylor Street. Duncan radioed in that the fight was on the north end, so I took the first road that turned in that direction. We flew up division, passing a few people who were moving south. I saw three women herding a group of small children, and they gave hopeful glances our way as we passed. I began to feel the old rage start to rise again and I gripped the wheel tighter.

At Lucas Street, I stopped and jumped out of the vehicle, grabbing my weapons as I went. I heard firing to the east, so I headed that way. In our world, shots meant someone was still alive, so rescues started in the general vicinity of flying bullets. Running in was risky, because in the heat of battle people didn't necessarily ask your pardon before they took a shot at you.

Charlie was right behind me, and Tommy and Duncan, close behind. Sarah and Rebecca were bringing up the truck and van, using them as high points to fire from should we need cover.

A short, younger looking man saw us coming over and he sprinted towards us.

"Who are you?" he panted. He was carrying a lever action rifle and had a small bag slung over his shoulder. As he sized us up, he took a moment to reach into the bag, extract a handful of bullets, and start loading them into the magazine of his gun.

"John Talon. Need help?" I kept it short.

"Hell, yes! Had an outbreak last night. No idea how the hell it got started. Suddenly, people woke up to zombies in their houses. We lost twenty three in the first attack, then forty more for sure when they left their homes and started hunting." He finished reloading and pointed the rifle to the east. "We've got people stuck in the post office, and we're not set up for this!" He started running back in the direction of the post office and we jogged to keep up. "I'm trying to get reinforcements, but we sent most people south to save kids!"

"How many are trapped?" I asked.

"About two dozen, and they're unarmed!" The man ran further and as we cleared Oak Street, I could see the Post Office.

I could also see the horde of zombies that had it surrounded. They were a nasty looking bunch, covered in bright blood and gore. They hadn't seen us, yet, and we could use that to our advantage if we kept our heads.

"Kill them!" Our guide opened up on the zombies and dropped one with five shots. At the firing, most of the zombies turned our way, a few turning and starting to stumble in our direction.

So much for keeping our heads. "Duncan, Tommy, let's split them up. Nothing fancy, let's just shoot them."

Tommy checked the safety on his rifle and nodded. "Got it." He and Duncan ran up the street a ways, drawing the attention of a number of zombies. About twenty started moving in their direction.

Charlie and I stepped away from the man with the lever gun and waited patiently. The zombies that had seen us were advancing, slightly faster than normal, which was to be guessed, seeing as how fresh they were. Our guide emptied his gun and grabbed another handful of cartridges from his bag. As he was reloading, the horde got closer and closer. A little bit of mental calculation figured the man would be dead before he managed to get his gun firing again.

"Close enough. Outside in?" Charlie asked.

"Works for me. I'll start with Fatty over there." I pointed with my rifle barrel a fat zombie making his way over. His entire shirtfront was covered in blood, and his jowls wobbled as he took each laborious step.

"Got it."

Charlie started firing on the right side of the horde and I started on the left. We worked our way deliberately from the edges, knocking down Z after Z. The ones we knocked down tripped the ones still coming, so our next line of firing was a bit more erratic as the zombies we were drawing a bead on suddenly fell from sight.

After putting down ten zombies, I checked on Duncan and Tommy's progress. They had put down as many as we had, and it looked like things were not going to be all that bad, here at least. Charlie had put down nearly the same amount, so we were in pretty good shape.

Fifteen minutes after we had arrived at the scene, Duncan put the last zombie away. I did a quick look around of the Post Office, and made sure we hadn't missed any, or there weren't any that might have been hiding in the tall grass.

I went back to my comrades. "That ought to do it. Tommy, you take the van and scout around the area, make sure there aren't any surprises waiting for these people when they go back to their homes. Duncan, you go with Sarah and check on the people to the south. Make sure they don't have any problems they need taking care of."

Tommy and Duncan nodded and were about to head back to the vehicles when Charlie stopped them. "Here," he said, handing them his rifle. "We should be done with the heavy stuff around here."

I thought that was a good idea, so I handed Tommy my rifle as well. No point in lugging the thing around when the threat was finished. When they had gone, I looked around and didn't see our guide. "Where'd he go?" I queried.

"Who?" Charlie asked.

"Our buddy."

"Oh, he's by the side door of the Post Office. Looks like he's trying to get in."

I looked over and saw the man was pulling at a door, trying to open it. He seemed kind of frantic, which I could understand, given the circumstances. He shouted something, listened at the door, and then started pounding on it. He listened again and then the door burst open, knocking him backwards and away from the building. Two dozen zombies spilled out, falling on the man and tearing at him with teeth and nails. He screamed once, and then went down in a heap of torn and bloody flesh. He was dead in seconds and several zombies knelt to feast while others clawed at the body, trying to tear off pieces, which they stuffed in bloody mouths.

"Jesus!" Charlie exclaimed, grabbing for his tomahawks.

I just stared, too stunned to speak. I pulled out my own 'hawk and my trusty pickaxe, too.

We stood still, unnoticed by the crowd that was surrounding and slobbering over the fallen man. Someone must have been bitten, and then they turned in the confines of the Post Office. Tough choice to make. Stay and be eaten, or go outside and be eaten.

CHAPTER 41

I finally found my voice. "Gee, I'm glad we gave away our rifles."

Charlie barked a small laugh, and then got serious as the zombies finally noticed us. "You want to take this head on?" he asked.

I shook my head. "Way too many of them, and they're too recently dead. They're too fast to let them surround us."

"Call it then, and let's get it over with," Charlie said.

"Gonna get some exercise. Outside in, keep moving. With luck, the others will get back and give us a hand." I hoped they would be back soon.

The crowd finally noticed us and started in our direction. The man they had eaten was little more than bits of flesh on bones. His face had been eaten off, and his organs had been ripped out and devoured. I hadn't seen that much destruction in a while. His arms and legs were eaten to the bone, and his head had been cracked on the sidewalk, preventing him from even attempting to come back.

"Well, here they come. Good luck." Charlie ducked away to the east, jogging around the edge of the horde. One zombie was slightly faster than the others were and managed to get in the way. Charlie backhanded his right tomahawk into the ghoul's temple, cracking its skull and causing its right eye to bulge out. Charlie didn't wait for it to fall, he just kept moving. As he passed the Zs, they turned to follow, bumping into each other in their eagerness to feed.

I took off to the west, working the edge of the crowd myself. I didn't have any quicker ones come out and say hello, so I was going to have to do it the hard way. I stepped in quickly, using the longer reach of my pickaxe to smack a large zombie above the ear, killing it and knocking it into its neighbor, who fell to the ground with the dead one.

I knew there were other ones coming up behind me, so I kept moving, and angling away from the crowd. Around the north end, I spiked another Z in the head, just as Charlie came into view. He stepped into the crowd, swinging with both hands and killing two at once. I waved at him and then reversed course, heading back the way I came. The horde had spread out a bit, giving me a few more solitary targets I could kill without serious risk to myself.

I cut down a woman with wild hair and a huge tear in her throat. Speeding up a little, I used the pointed end of my 'hawk to finish off a small man reaching for my arms.

I stayed on the outskirts of the horde, killing as they came out, and my movement kept the zombies off focus and continuously bumping into each other.

On the south end of the zombies, Charlie had to make a stand and take on three at once. He kicked the middle one in the hip, and slammed his right hand 'hawk into the forehead of the one on the left, letting it go as the Z fell. The right one died as Charlie buried the second blade in its neck, severing its spine. Charlie jerked it free, as the ghoul fell, bringing it back for a two handed swing into the skull of the one trying to get up. Charlie grabbed his weapons and backed away, working his way towards the North again.

I didn't have time to admire Charlie's skills, as two bore down on me with little room for guessing as to their intent. A back handed swing with my left hand brought the spike end of my tomahawk into the forehead of the smaller zombie, who managed to rip it out of my grasp as he fell backwards. I swung my pick at the second one, but I misjudged the distance and only managed to rap it on the noggin with the handle. The zombie lunged forward, but I ducked under its outstretched arms, keeping a grip on my pick. I hooked the Z behind the neck with the pickaxe and brought the weapon around, spinning the zombie to the ground. As I brought the pick back for a swing, I caught another zombie coming at me out of the corner of my eye. Twisting awkwardly, I managed to swing the pointed end of the pick at the Z. catching him right above the temple.

I stepped back to give myself some room, and just managed to avoid getting bitten by the zombie on the ground that had crawled forward for a bite. I slammed my axe onto his head, killing him instantly. I had to move, otherwise, I was going to get swamped in a hurry, so I dodged the arms of an attractive zombie, at least she would have been if her nose were still on her face.

I circled back to the north and killed another one, this one was an older, grey haired gent. At the far end, Charlie and I exchanged pleasantries and returned the way we came. I was starting to wonder where the hell everyone else was, as this was getting tiresome. These zombies were fresh, which meant they were harder to kill. Older zombies reach a level of decay that makes for more brittle bones and skulls. At some point, they stop decaying, but we haven't figured out the why of that. New zombies took serious swings to crack their skulls.

At the south end, I decided to get this over with, as we had killed the majority and there were only about fifteen left. I could see Charlie working his way back, his tomahawk flashing and killing, when disaster struck. Charlie was ten feet away from me, and I was getting ready to kill another zombie, when he suddenly tripped. All I could see was he was upright, and then he was down. I swung extra hard and buried the pick end of my weapon in the head of the zombie that was coming at me, a shirtless man with huge bites out of his arms.

"Hang on!" I raced over to Charlie, as he was struggling to get to his feet. One of the zombies that he thought he had killed had just enough strength left to grab Charlie's foot. A large man with a torn face was bearing down on Charlie, and I managed to intercept him just in time. I jammed my forearm under the Zs chin, forcing his head up and away. The zombie was still strong and managed to resist being pushed back. I got a full face of zombie breath as I snarled back into the grim visage.

As always, the eyes of the zombie were the most disturbing. I could handle the wounds and the decay, I expected that. But the eyes, the windows to the soul, were the creepiest part. On older zombies, it wasn't so bad. Their eyes were kind of milky and you couldn't see them well. But on the new zombies, the eyes were clear and dead. There was nothing behind them. They were truly and completely dead. We've had people tell us that the zombies might actually still be alive, but if they ever took a look into the eyes of a zombie, they would know those things are very dead.

I shoved harder and heard Charlie curse behind me. Other zombies were closing in on three sides, and I was running out of time and room to work my weapons.

"Screw it." I pulled my pistol, while the zombie clawed at my arms and shoulders, trying to pull me in for a bite. I shoved the barrel into the Zs left eye and sent his last thoughts out the back of his head. The zombie fell backwards and I quickly lined up the next three, dropping them quickly. Charlie finally managed to free himself, and he pulled his weapon as well. In a short amount of time, we blew away the last of the zombies.

As the last one fell, and the sound of the pistol report drifted away, I looked over at Charlie and shook my head.

"I keep feeling like we're somehow responsible for this," I said, wiping off my weapons and putting them back where they belong.

Charlie nodded. "I feel the same way. Maybe we just need to hard charge to the next undisturbed settlement and get their defenses up."

"That sounds good, but are we then condemning the ones we passed by to death. If the people don't know what they're up against, they're going to get creamed."

"Didn't think of that. Any more luck on figuring out how these towns are connected?"

"Still not seeing it. The only link I have is the roads, and we've been on the roads they would have used. It doesn't make sense." I started walking south to see if there were any additional problems, we might encounter. As we moved further south, I could see some activity here and there. Some zombies were still around, but since we had wiped out the main horde, people were much less fearful to attack and were taking care of the remaining zombies.

Two blocks from our fight, the truck and van came careening around a corner. When they saw us, the two vehicles came to a screeching halt. Several zombies turned at the noise, and the townsfolk used the opportunity of distraction to kill the ghouls in front of them.

Sarah leaned her head out the window. "We gotta go! Another town is under attack and they need help!"

My shoulders slumped. "Jesus Christ! This is getting tedious." I turned to Charlie. "We may have to make one of those hard decisions if we're to get ahead of this."

Charlie nodded as he moved to the van. "It's what we do."

I thought about that as I got into the truck. It was what we did, whether we liked it or not.

CHAPTER 42

I shook myself out of my wandering thoughts and grabbed the map. "What town?"

"According to Duncan, it's the town of Afton," Sarah said, gunning the engine and swerving out of town. She picked up Route 34 again and headed east, trusting her instincts that it was the correct way to go.

I found the town we were in and started looking to the east. I found Afton a ways in, and whistled. I grabbed the radio in response to Sarah's querulous look.

"Duncan! Come in! Over!" Time was short.

"Duncan here. What's up?"

"What's the situation in Afton? Over." I hoped it was stable.

"Not good. An outbreak surprised them, and they're running out of options. The survivors are holed up in a school, but they're having trouble keeping the Zs out. They didn't have time to prepare any defenses." Duncan didn't sound hopeful.

I hated my next question. "How many people are we talking about?" Sarah looked sharply at me and I didn't answer her visual rebuke.

Duncan took a minute to answer. "They say there's fifteen trapped in the school, with about ninety zombies trying to get in."

I took a long time to answer. "All right, we'll see what we're about. At 169, head south, that should take us to the middle of town. The school should be around there somewhere. John out."

Sarah pushed the vehicle a little faster. "For a minute there, I thought you were going to say skip it." Her voice was quiet, like she gets when she knows she's going to get an answer she didn't like.

I stared out the window, watching the hills roll by. "I almost did. But I have enough ghosts around me. I don't need any more." I did, too. Everyone I couldn't save, everyone I had to leave behind, and everyone I lost to the Upheaval and the Zombie Wars. They came during the quiet times, staying just out of sight, but I knew they were there. All I could do was ask for forgiveness.

Sarah reached out and put a hand on leg. "You do what you do, John. Someone has to make the hard choices."

Somehow, that didn't make me feel any better. "I didn't want this mission at all, remember? I wanted to let it go, give it to the army, just live in peace and quiet."

Sarah was sharper in her response. "Get real, John. The army would still be trying to get out here, and by the time they figured things out, that group would be at the river, trying to figure a way across. We'd have come home to nothing but death. Do you think your brother could hold off this horde by himself?"

I had to admit she had a point. Mike was good enough, but the crowd would overwhelm him in no time. I wasn't even sure the cougars could handle them.

"All right." I conceded. "All right. Let's get those people out of there and then get ourselves ahead of this mess. We won't stay to kill off the new ones, we'll just send the survivors to the last town and they can get a group together to deal with them."

"Good plan." Sarah smiled.

I had to chuckle a little myself. This was one of those times going back all the way to when Sarah and I first got together that I realized no matter what anyone said, I really wasn't in charge.

Sarah moved as fast as she could down the road, managing to keep us from blowing any tires, but going as quickly as possible. It was nerve-wracking, knowing there were survivors who knew we were coming, but they had to wait while the zombies, friends and family they knew were infected, tried their best to eat them alive.

Fifteen minutes later, we turned down Route 169 in a roar of gravel and gears. I actually had to hold on, while Sarah grimly guided the truck.

Afton was a small community with a dwindling population. Even before the end of the world, the population was only three hundred, according to the map stats. We flew down the street, and I happened to see a sign for a school crossing. Craning my neck, I saw a low building in the distance.

"Ahead on the right!" I called out, radioing to the van that we were about to go hot.

"Got it!" Sarah saw what I was looking at and drove faster, swerving around a couple of flatbed wagons sitting in the road. I checked my weapons and unfastened my seatbelt.

Let us be in time, I prayed silently, grabbing the door handle for a quick exit. The trees and streets zipped past, and then the school was suddenly on our right. Sarah braked quickly, but avoided squealing the tires. I hopped out of the truck and grabbed up my rifle, chambering a round and bringing it to bear in the direction of the school.

There were dozens of zombies milling about the property, and I almost started shooting, when I saw something that made my heart sink. The front door of the school was smashed in, and the zombies were slowly shuffling into the school. The unhurried nature of the zombies told me there was no one left alive in the school.

Charlie came up beside me and he saw the same thing I did. "Damn."

I had nothing to add. "Yeah."

"We going to go?" Charlie asked, indicating the zombies that had seen us and were moving in our direction.

"May as well, there's nothing here to..." My voice trailed off as I saw movement on the roof. "Up there! They're alive!" I shouted. Several figures had stood up from where they were lying, in the hopes that the zombies would eventually drift away and they could escape.

Charlie gestured to the van and Rebecca moved it into position. Tommy and Duncan came and stood beside us. The zombies, hearing my voice, began their moaning and shuffling. Inside the building, other zombies took up the call, telling the world outside that hell was just a little bite away.

I took that groan as a challenge. Sighting in the closest zombie, I muttered, "Not today." I fired and heard four more rifles firing right after me. This one we win, I thought.

We didn't waste any time with hand-to-hand combat. We just shot them dead. The ones outside quickly piled up, and when they were wiped out, Rebecca brought the van over to the side of the building where Charlie and myself helped the people of the town come down off the roof. Tommy, Duncan and Sarah cleared out the building and declared it clean.

I stood on the ground with a younger man, shaking his hand and waving away his thanks.

"You did well, all things considered," I said. "I doubt another town would have made it at all."

The man, whose name was Louis Norman, just shrugged. "Not sure how well I did. When I saw things were really bad, I just yelled out for anyone who was alive to follow me."

"It worked, but it looks like most of your town is gone. Sorry we couldn't get here sooner."

"Hey, I'm glad you made it at all. Any idea what hit us?"

I told him about the little zombies and that they were acting in a way that was totally new. They were attacking towns, but not sticking around to eat. It was mostly just hit and run. They attacked when they had the numbers, but retreated when a superior force confronted them. We had no idea how they were getting from town to town, and we were afraid they would break through everyone's defenses and leave us with a mess everywhere we went. I really had no desire to relive the Upheaval.

Louis looked over his little band, and the piles of zombies that used to be his friends and family, and shuddered. "What a mess," he said quietly. A little louder, he said, "If you need to get moving, don't worry about us. We've got enough vehicles to spare and we're sure not going to stick around here."

I nodded as Duncan spoke up. "I'll radio ahead and let them know you're coming, and I'll let them know what happened here."

Louis nodded. "I'm obliged to you."

I hated to save and run, but we had to move quickly. "All right then. Good luck. Glad we could help."

Louis shook all of our hands, and then went back to his little group. We climbed aboard our truck and van and moved out quickly. Behind us, in the mirror, I could see the remains of the townspeople poking among the dead. Some kneeling beside fallen loved ones, others heading off to homes that would never be homes again.

CHAPTER 43

Noon found us at Murphy, a small town just a little out of the way. It was a tiny little side stop, barely a footnote on the map. The town consisted of ten streets that went east and west, and ten streets that went north and south. All told, it was neatly tucked into a half square mile of Iowa landscape.

It was also completely abandoned. There were no occupied houses, and if I had to guess, the homes might have been abandoned even before the Upheaval. The only business I could immediately see was a grain elevator by the railroad tracks and various small businesses and local bars. The favorite color for homes seemed to be white, because they were all over the place. We drove through slowly, taking in the quaint town, and I found myself wondering what it might have been like had the end of the world not occurred. There were several Victorian-style homes, and they looked to have been well maintained, if needing a coat of paint.

"Penny for your thoughts," Sarah said, breaking me out of my reflections.

I shook my head to clear it a little. "Just trying to figure out how these little suckers are operating. This is a level of sophistication we've never encountered before, and we're just trying like hell to keep up." I looked out the window again as more of the small town drifted by. "I wish I knew where they were going next."

Sarah maneuvered her way around a truck parked in the middle of the road, deftly avoiding a kid's bike, and moving the truck to head back to the route we were following. "I know. Part of me wants to just floor it and get to the river, but we need to try to get ahead to warn the towns."

"I wish our radios had longer range, but I might as well wish for a rocket-propelled chain-saw launcher while I'm at it," I said.

Sarah mentally chewed on that one for a while. "Might be possible," she murmured.

I just smiled to myself.

We got our first break when we drove as fast as we could to the next town, which was Osceola. Osceola was a different town, in that it was one of the few to weather the Upheaval without any serious problems. They were located far enough from Des Moines that they did not suffer the influx of infected refugees from a large city, and they managed to contain what little infection they had pretty well. When the big mess hit, everyone in Osceola stayed indoors, locked in their own homes. If someone got sick, they were contained, and if they got out, they didn't infect anyone else. It was interesting that the biggest problem Osceola had in the aftermath was trying to feed all of the people who survived the Upheaval.

Sarah pulled the truck up to the edge of the town, and a man on a horse rode over to greet us. He was armed with a scoped rifle, and it was plain to see he was quite competent with it.

"Howdy!" he called. He was a decent-looking fellow, wearing a plain jacket and jeans. A wide brimmed hat covered his head and bright blue eyes looked our gear and us over. "How might I help you folks?"

Sarah spoke before I did. "We're from the capital, chasing down a series of outbreaks. They've been headed this way, and we were wondering if you have had any trouble here."

The man's face changed when Sarah used the word outbreak, which was normal for the times we lived in. "Outbreak? No, it's been quiet around here. Outbreak, huh?" The man looked to the west trying to see if there was anything out there that might warn him of danger.

I spoke up. "I'm not going to lie, this one is bad." I told him about the little zombies and their propensity to kill and run, letting the dead do their dirty work for them. I let them know what happened to the last town, and we were glad to see that this one had at least been spared.

The man nodded. "Well, if you folks don't mind, I'm going to ride in and raise the alarm. We'll get some people out here to keep an eye on things, and everyone will button up tight for a while. Name's Ken Barnes, by the way." The man held out his hand.

I shook his outstretched hand. "John Talon." With my other hand, I patted the chestnut mare he was riding.

Ken looked at me for a second. "Heard of you. Obliged." He turned the horse quickly and expertly rode the animal over the uneven terrain, heading into town.

Sarah looked at me and I shrugged. "Guess we should roll in and see if we can lend a hand."

Sarah shrugged back and we rolled into the town. The word seemed to have spread quickly, as there was a lot of activity. People were moving about, carrying water and food to various places, and we saw several men on horseback riding out to the plains beyond the town. At first, I wasn't sure what the point of that was, but I figured they must have that response when there was any kind of danger. It made sense to go out and meet the enemy, even though you ran the risk of infection. At least, it was away from the town.

At the town hall, I met with a man who was the mayor, and he directed me to the communications center. I spent five minutes on the radio, relaying a message to be sent to the capital regarding what we were facing, and what we would probably be needing. I left the message that the army needed to be out on the river and be patrolling between Burlington and Keithsburg. It was a large order, but we still didn't know where these little monsters were. I hoped they got the message in time.

My duty done, I watched the activity around me for a minute, and then Charlie came up beside me. The sun was starting to set, and I was back in survival mode enough to figure we needed to find a place to spend the night. I was hoping this would be our last night in Iowa, but I learned a long time ago that timetables were useless unless you wanted to frustrate yourself.

"What's the next move? Are we going to help out here?" Charlie asked. Behind him, the rest of the crew was out of the vehicles, stretching and working out cramps.

I shook my head. "I think the best move would be to get on the outside, get ourselves to the next town, and set up for the night. If we've gotten ahead of this, then we need to warn the towns north and south. We know this little bunch of Zs will avoid a fight they might lose, so they might head off into the weeds and we're right back where we started."

"Sounds like a plan, although it kind of feels weird to pull away from a fight." Charlie rotated his head, popping his neck.

"I know. But they've survived before, and this time they know what's coming, if it comes here at all." I watched several men go by and they all looked grim and determined. I understood their concern. There were a lot of people and that could become a lot of zombies really fast if they weren't diligent.

"Let's get ourselves out of the way and decide where we want to head for the night," I said as I went back to the truck. Sarah was sitting on the edge of the truck bed, her legs dangling over the side. She gave me a wink as I strolled up, and I wondered what she was up to, but didn't have the time to ask.

"Okay, here's the situation." I started, waving Duncan and Tommy over. They were talking to a man who gave them a small sack, then jogged away. The two moved over, and as I talked, handed out some homemade peanut brittle.

"As far as we know, this place is next in line to be attacked, and they are as ready as they are ever going to be," I said, around a mouth of sticky brittle. "We're going to head out and see about getting our warning to some towns to the north and south. If we can get this coordinated, we might be able to return the favor and attack the zombies."

Charlie raised his eyebrows. "Won't we have to be attacked to know where the little bastards are?"

Tommy spoke up. "Unfortunately, yes. But if the guys on the radios are sharp, then surrounding towns can move in, cutting off a run by the zombies."

Rebecca chimed in. "Seems pretty thin. We don't even know how those things are advancing, and we're trying to be on the lookout for them?"

I raised my hands. "I'm open to ideas. I'd be halfway home by now if I had my choice."

Sarah saved me by her suggestion. "Why don't we head east, and then head north until we can radio the next town. Then we head south until we can do the same. The best thing we can do is warn people, and then those things can be killed piecemeal."

The rest of the crew nodded, and we piled into the vehicles to get moving. As we left, there were a lot of curious lances, but no one challenged us or tried to stop us. I guess they were used to dealing with things on their own.

I looked at the map, and saw that the closest town was Woodburn. We'd head in that direction, and then hit Lucas. After that, we'd have to choose which direction we wanted to go to first, and hope for the best.

CHAPTER 44

Back on the road, Sarah drove for a bit, and then asked, "Where do you want to spend the night?" She pointed to the darkening sky as we headed east.

I grabbed the map, looked at it for a moment, and then shrugged. "Let's see what we can find in Woodburn. Lucas can wait until morning."

We drove for a while, and then turned south when we saw the sign for the town of Woodburn. I didn't expect much for the town, given the sign boasted a thriving population of three hundred people. However, one never knew, and we were headed there anyway.

A half hour before dark fall, we pulled into the town. Right away, we knew we weren't going to have any trouble finding accommodations, since it seemed they had been out of business for a long time. The town was dilapidated and old, and once again, for the life of me, I couldn't decide if they had abandoned the town before or after it became an issue for the dead to decide.

We passed home after home, and the thing that stuck out to me was there wasn't any evidence of hurried abandonment. No belongings in the streets, no open doors, no open garage doors. Several of the homes had wood barring the windows and doors, but nothing on the inside, suggesting the owners might have had notions of eventually returning. I could relate, since I had done the same in what seemed like a lifetime ago.

"Where should we stop?" Sarah asked, moving the truck down one street, then the next. The homes were widely spaced, and it gave a lot of room for growing families a lot of room to spend outdoors.

"How about at a business? I always feel weird sleeping in someone else's bedroom or living room." I looked around for some sign of a business district, but nothing stood out.

"Me, too. Especially when you start to feel frisky," Sarah teased.

"Me? Need I remind you of the time we were in Cheyenne and you thought the western wear store was 'romantic'?" I said.

Sarah grinned mischievously. "Forgot about that."

"Yeah. Three hundred zombies at the door and you were playing cowgirl, because you found a hat."

"I don't recall you complaining," Sarah pouted.

"Who's complaining? I'm just pointing out the fact that you have your share of 'moments'."

"All right, all right," Sarah laughed. "Find us a place to put up for the night and I might feel frisky myself."

I was immediately interested in the town and looked very hard for a defendable place to spend the night. I don't know why, but I didn't want to be anywhere that had more than two ways in.

Down the street, I saw a couple of large buildings. Turning the corner, I saw that the two were competing bars. I say competing, because it was a close contest as to which one looked seedier. The southern one, called the Whitebreast Inn, sported a sign that had a woman whose attributes defied gravity. The other one, called the Double D, had another anatomically freakish female flaunting her wares.

"You're kidding." Sarah looked at the two buildings and shook her head.

"Think tactically," I said, grinning. "There are no windows, two exits, and chances are they're soundproof because of the location in town."

"You're insane." Sarah looked the two places over dubiously. "All right, it's on you to clear them, but if there are any stripper zombies in there, you're on your own."

"Deal." I hopped out of the cab of the truck and went over to the van. Charlie was just shaking his head at me while Rebecca waggled a finger. Tommy and Duncan practically fell out of the van, and I could see Duncan was full of his usual silliness.

"Oh, man," Duncan said. "I need some singles! Anyone got change for a ten?"

We all laughed as we approached the door of the Double D, and Duncan paused to run a finger over the photographed cleavage of a spotlighted dancer.

"All right, let's see what we got." I pulled out my pistol and aimed it at the door. Tommy grabbed the handle and gave it a small jerk. The door was locked, which was actually a positive sign. It increased the chances the place was empty.

Charlie swung his pack around and rummaged a bit. In a minute, he had a lock-picking tool that was originally intended for car doors. We found it worked well on lots of locked doors.

This one was no exception. In a second, the door was unlocked and we stepped inside. The interior was dark everywhere, with dark wood, dark carpeting, and darkly painted walls and ceiling. The main area had three runways and three stripper poles, with two cages for dancers by the bar. The bar ran along the entire wall and there was a small door with the letters VIP written on it.

Tommy checked out the back room, while Duncan checked out the area behind the stage. I went behind the bar to the manager's office and Charlie checked out the storage area.

In five minutes, we met back at the center stage. Duncan twirled around the tall pole in the center.

"All clear backstage," he said, spinning.

"VIP area clear. Just a bunch of couches and a small bar," Tommy said.

"Manager's office clear, nothing of use in there," I said.

"Found a nice loft in the storage area, has a good window that looks out over the town," Charlie said.

"Okay, then," I said. Let's check out the Whitebreast Inn."

Duncan jumped off the stage. "Thought you'd never ask."

We stepped outside and threw a wave to the ladies as we sauntered over to the Inn. This time the door was open, and we prepped ourselves a little better than the last time.

Going in, it was clear this place had been empty for a while, and its layout was completely different from the other. In this place, you stepped up to an elevated platform that went around the entire building. There was a backstage area, which was walled off, and then a balcony that went around the upper part of the building. Small café-style tables and chairs lined the balcony, and they was a small bar area directly above where we were standing.

"Oh, man," Duncan said.

"What? Oh. That's too bad," said Tommy.

Charlie looked over at what they were staring at and just shook his head.

"Damn." My contribution to the conversation was just as deep as the others, but it encompassed a wide range of emotions.

Hanging from the balcony, with varying implements used for the deed, were seven corpses. They were all women, and by the looks of them, they had been pretty when they were alive. However, for whatever reason, either someone had killed them or they decided to end it all together, they were hanging motionless over the bar where they had probably worked together

I tapped the others on the shoulders and we made our way back out. That bar was their tomb, and we were disturbing them. I didn't need any more ghosts on my ass right now.

Heading back to Sarah, I filled them in on the buildings, and the women agreed we should leave the Whitebreast Inn alone. We parked the Truck near the front of the building and the van near the back. Inside, Charlie and Rebecca took over the VIP room, while Sarah and I claimed the loft. Tommy grabbed the sofa in the manager's office, and Duncan decided he was going to stay in the van and monitor the radio for any developments.

Up in the loft, I stretched out on the floor and used my backpack as a pillow. Sarah took her time taking off her weapons, and somehow she made that look good.

"Hey you," I said quietly.

"Hey yourself," she said back. Settling down next to me, Sarah snuggled in close and asked. "Do you think Jake and Aaron are okay?"

I felt guilty that I hadn't really thought about the two of them in a while, but I nodded. "They're fine. Probably driving Mike nuts by now."

"When do you think we'll be back?"

"I figure three days at the most. The army should be on its way, and will hit the border by the day after tomorrow. We just need to stay ahead of the zombies and we should be okay."

Sarah changed topics. "How do you think they're getting around without anyone seeing them?"

I shrugged slightly. "Wish to hell I knew. We may know more if Osceola gets hit. Hopefully, they will be able to knock them back then track their movements so we can set up a trap. Get some sleep."

Sarah lifted her head up. "You're tired?"

I pulled her close. "Not that tired."

CHAPTER 45

In the morning, I woke up stiff and sore. I hadn't slept on a floor in a long time, and my back was reminding me that I wasn't as young as I used to be. Add to the fact that, Sarah and I might have gotten a bit aggressive last night, my elbows and knees were banged up as well.

I stretched out the kinks in my back and moved over to my gear. I took out a bottle of water and put a little on a small towel to wash the sleep off of me. As I rubbed down my face and arms, I looked at the scars I had accumulated over the years. Some I wore with honor, like the scar I got from Thorton. Others I would just as soon forget, like the one I got across my hand from a training exercise gone very wrong.

Sarah stirred and the sunlight from the window fell across her head and shoulders, illuminating her bare back and arms. She brought her legs up and the blanket pulled away, revealing a landscape of smooth skin and curves.

I was extremely tempted to head back under the blanket for a really good morning when I glanced out the window. A slight movement caught my eye, and I stepped closer to the glass, looking out at the quiet town.

"Holy fucking shit." The words were out of my mouth before I realized it, and it caused Sarah to turn again, this time covering herself.

"What's up? Good morning, by the way." Sarah stretched luxuriously, all the way to her little toes sticking out of bottom of the blanket. I nearly forgot what was outside.

I pulled away from the window and moved quickly to our gear. I started putting my clothes on when Sarah rolled over again, laying on her stomach. Her bare bottom peeked out at me from behind her head, and her elbows propping her head and shoulders up emphasized her breasts.

"Why are you getting dressed? I was hoping to get a little more of what we had last night." Sarah pouted and I damn near relented.

"Would love to, just as soon as the hundreds of little zombies outside our door pass us by," I whispered.

Sarah's eyes got wide and she jumped to her feet, giving me heart palpitations as parts of her bounced very nicely. She dressed as quickly as I did, and in a minute, we were back to our dangerous selves. We crept over to the window and looking carefully out, we surveyed the scene before us.

Dozens of zombie children moved along the street, stepping quickly past the strip club and heading up Sigler Street. There was a long procession of the deadly little things and they were moving quickly. I couldn't see what was leading them, there were too many for that, but they walked along the road in nearly single file fashion, one child after another. It was as if they were moving from classroom to classroom in an elementary building.

"Do you think they know we're here?" Sarah asked, fingering her supply of magazines.

"Don't know, doubt it, though." I looked at their line of travel, cursing the luck that put us on the west side of the building. If we could see out the east, we could see the leader, if there was one, and where they were actually going.

I watched for a bit, and then gave Sarah a quick kiss. "I'm going down to warn the rest. I hope to hell Duncan came in from the van last night."

"Oh, God."

I hurried down the stairs as quietly as I could and raced for the dance floor. If those little things knew we were here, they would be on us like no one's business. In the manager's office, I roused Tommy and let him know what was going on. His sleepy answers turned to whispered curses as he struggled to get himself up.

I went to the VIP area and as I approached, I heard Rebecca giggle. I shook my head, realizing my friend was doing what I wish I could do at this moment. Guess they just got up earlier than Sarah did and I did.

I tried to knock discreetly on the wall, but it was hard since everything was covered in carpet. I tried whispering, but I couldn't get past the noises that were coming from the room.

Finally, I had to resort to direct methods, so I took a magazine from my holder and tossed it into the room, hoping to get lucky.

"Ow! What the hell?" Charlie said.

Apparently, I got luckier than I thought. I stepped back from the curtain just as it was pulled aside. A very angry and very naked Charlie James swept the curtain back and glared out at me, holding my magazine. A red spot was forming on his forehead. A glance at my attire and he changed his expression.

"John."

"Charlie."

"Trouble?"

"Lots."

"Be ready in two minutes."

"Come up to the loft."

"Will do. Your magazine."

"Thanks." We never broke eye contact during the exchange, and I grinned after Charlie drew the curtain back across the threshold. That will be one we never talk about. I thought.

Back at the loft, Sarah was watching the procession of zombies streaming past the building. We didn't know where they were going, but this was a big break. Up until now, we had been guessing where they were and trying to predict where they were going to strike next. Suddenly, they were right in front of us, and we could easily track them and guide the army to a point where they could be decimated.

I looked out the window. "How many do you figure?" I whispered, watching the line go by.

"About one hundred fifty that I've seen. Probably a lot more has passed us by," Sarah said.

"Do you think Duncan is up and knows to keep quiet?" I asked, looking down at the van below us.

"Hope so, or we'll never see him again," Sarah said ominously.

I understood what she meant. If he stumbled out of that van while the zombies were mobbing past, they'd be on him before he even knew they were there. The only reassurance we had for his survival was the fact Duncan was an old campaigner, and wouldn't likely make such a rookie mistake. Sure, he was a goof, but he was as solid as they come and there was no quit in the man.

Charlie and Rebecca silently came up to the loft, and Sarah and I made room for them to see out the window. When Rebecca looked at me, her cheeks colored slightly, and Sarah picked up on it right away. She pulled me away to look into our packs and confronted me with our backs turned to Charlie and Rebecca.

"Did you walk in on them?" Sarah chided.

I nodded. "But not as bad as you think. I was behind a curtain, and they couldn't hear me, so I threw a magazine at them."

Sarah groaned softly. "Oh, no! Who did you hit? Rebecca?"

"I didn't!" I protested. "I swear I did not hit Rebecca with a magazine."

"Good."

"I hit Charlie in the head."

"John!"

"Shhh!"

We turned back to the window as Charlie let out a slow whistle. "Damn." Was all he said.

Tommy came up the stairs a minute later, and he looked out the window at the procession of zombies.

"There's just something so wrong about this," he whispered, watching the zombie kids go by. Since a lot of them were relatively new, they looked almost normal. The thing that gave them away, however, was the dark red circles around their eyes. That and the bloodstains on their shirts and chins. The older ones, the ones that must have come from the school, were the very white ones. These had older, thinner clothing and lankier hair. I thought it strange that they weren't grey like the old ones we encountered now and then.

The line thinned out and the last zombie walked away towards the east, around the building and out of our sight. We all breathed a sigh of relief, only to replace it with a gasp of surprise when Duncan opened the side of the van, the one facing the retreating zombies.

"John! Wake up! Osceola is under attack!" Duncan looked at the line of zombies that had suddenly stopped to turn and look at him. In a lower voice, we could hear Duncan say, "Aaannnd... so are we."

CHAPTER 46

Duncan spun around and dove into the van, slamming the door shut just as five little zombies crashed against it. They bounced off and backed away, circling the van as others came back to investigate. They kept their distance, which was very weird, but none of this fit anything we knew. Right now, it looked like they knew the van could keep them out, but they weren't going anywhere, so they could wait for the meal in the box to get hungry or careless.

We couldn't wait for the zombies to win. "Tommy, get on the roof! Charlie, see if you can get to the truck out front and get to our heavier guns. They don't know we're here, so let's keep that element of surprise. Rebecca, you and Sarah stay here until Charlie and I get back with the guns. Find your best targets and keep an eye in their behavior."

"What are we looking for?" Sarah asked, peering out at the zombies that had begun to circle the van and slowly move around it. They were clicking their teeth together as they walked, some kind of sign they had spotted their prey and had run it to ground.

"Anything that gives us a clue to their behavior. Are they pack animals of a type, are they capable of some form of communication? Do they have any way of recognizing danger? What kind of intelligence do they have? Can they solve problems? Something, anything." I ran down the stairs without waiting for an answer and caught up to Charlie.

We stood by the front door and looked out carefully through the windows. Thanks to the heavily tinted glass, we could see out much better than they could see in. Way off to the east, we could see a convergence of zombies that watched while the others circled the van. In the far back of the pack, I could see a taller female standing and watching. She seemed to turn her head to the left and right, almost as if she were sniffing the air. She opened her mouth, but I couldn't tell if she made a noise. All I knew was five little zombies detached from the group and started to trot over to where the van was. We watched them pass by, and then the group turned and disappeared into the brush. They looked like they were heading south, but from where we were that was impossible to confirm.

"Did you see that?" Charlie asked quietly.

"I did," I said, pulling my pistol from my belt. "They can communicate and they have a leader."

"What the hell, John?" Charlie seemed almost in a panic. "How do we fight this? How do we go up against an enemy that's never going to tire, can figure a way around our defenses, is faster than anything we've seen, and can coordinate attacks?"

"Wish we had a choice, my friend, but the good news is we know they can die, and they run from a fight they can't win." I put a hand on the door, but Charlie stopped me.

"What if they don't run this time? Remember they kept coming when we put up a fight at the silos and I got bitten," Charlie said.

I thought about everything we had done, and how hard we had tried to put the world back on the right track. I thought about my sons and what they meant to me and what I was willing to do for them. The cold fire began to build, and I looked hard at Charlie.

"Then, by God, they will wish they had run, right before I put a bullet in them."

I stepped carefully outside, keeping an eye out for the five that had come to reinforce the ones surrounding the van. Fortunately, they had gone around the side of the building, so we were pretty good to go. I moved to the truck and pulled out my rifle, Sarah's rifle, and some extra ammo. Charlie kept a watch on the brush where we saw the rest disappear, but they seemed to be gone. He had holstered his gun, and held a sharp tomahawk in each hand. I understood his caution. A shot might attract all of the ones by the van, and we wanted to keep them in one place so we could get rid of them in one swoop.

As I closed the door of the truck, a little zombie came around the corner. He was a boy of about eight years old, roughly the same size as Jake, with sandy hair and blue eyes. His shirt was torn around the neck, and a raw bite wound could be seen in the same area. That was where the resemblance to anything we'd ever encountered ended.

This child's face was twisted with fury and pain, and his eyes burned at us. His small hands were claws, and they were black with what could only have been dried blood. When he saw us, his mouth pulled into a vicious leer, and he let out what could only be described as a combination of a growl, a snarl, and oddly, a meow.

The boy took a step forward, and then pitched onto his face as a tomahawk crashed into his forehead, right above his left eye. The blade had sunk in nearly to the haft, so Charlie must have put some serious force behind it. I knew then just how jumpy Charlie was.

As Charlie retrieved his 'hawk, I took the rifles inside. I waited for Charlie and we went up to the loft together. We didn't have much to say. We were both kind of lost in our own thoughts. Back in the loft, we relayed to the women what we had seen, and they gave us the rundown of what was going on around the van.

"They've circled a bit, and then they settled into three areas," Sarah said. "There's four right below us, another two in the shadows over by the shed, and three in front of the van. A single one wandered off towards the front of the building..."

"It found Charlie and me," I interrupted.

"One less to worry about," Sarah finished.

I got on the radio. "Tommy, what have you got?"

A minute later came the reply. "There's a bunch of them waiting beyond the trees to the east, looks like they might be waiting for this crew to catch up. Don't see any activity, they're just waiting."

"Can you get a shot at the leader?" I wanted to take out that anomaly as quickly as I could. This was just strange.

"Not on my best day. It's easily four hundred yards and all I have are open sights."

I looked over at Sarah and Rebecca and they both shook their heads.

"Our scoped rifles are in the van," Sarah said. "We'd just be lobbing bullets at this range."

I thought for a minute. "Tommy, do you have a shot at all against the ones near us?"

The reply wasn't encouraging. "Don't have a rifle. Could do it with my pistol, but I can't see them any better from here and when they see me, they'll run."

I signed off and stared out the window. Sarah watched my face for a second, and Charlie took his cue from Sarah.

My eyes narrowed and I looked out the window briefly.

"Aw, crap," Charlie said.

CHAPTER 47

"Let's go. Sarah, you and Rebecca open up from up here when we signal. Charlie, I'm going for the four under the window and you take the three by the shed. Just blow them away. Don't bother with headshots, just get them down and we'll finish them off. "

Charlie and I ran down the stairs and back to the front. We looked cautiously out and still didn't see anything. But we knew they were out there, waiting. Trouble was, they had time, and we didn't.

"Offense?" Charlie asked, putting a magazine in his hand for a faster reload.

"No choice and we have the element of surprise. Hopefully, when the girls open up, they won't scatter right into our laps," I said, putting a magazine reload in my hand as well.

"Christ, did you have to tell me that?" Charlie said.

"Hell, man, I'm making this up as I go. Those little fuckers defy everything I've seen with zombies."

We stepped outside and slowly made our way to the edge of the building. I wasn't sure if the ones by the shed were going to be able to see us or not, but I was grateful that the sun was throwing our shadows against the building, so we didn't have to worry about alerting them that way.

Charlie and I made our way towards the back wall, and by the time we got halfway there, I was sweating. The air was cool in the early autumn morning in Iowa, but I was sweating as if it was August in Florida. A quick glance back showed Charlie was in the same shape, and in all honesty, who could blame us? We were about to engage fast, smart zombies that could overwhelm us in a heartbeat. Charlie and maybe I could handle a bite at a time, but even our systems could be overloaded from multiple bites. It wasn't something I was willing to try out at this particular time.

At the edge of the building, I signaled to Charlie and he nodded. Reaching for my radio, I pressed the transmit button three times. I counted to three, and then stepped out into the open, moving away from the building.

Just as I came into sight, Sarah and Rebecca opened up from the window. Immediately there was chaos. Two forms fell to the ground in front of the van, while the rest looked up in shock at the windows where the shots came from. In that instant, I opened up on the four hitting one in the head and the other in the neck, slamming them both to the ground. The others bolted from the building and darted around towards the front of the van, joining the others as they moved away from the windows which were killing them. The three by the shed were knocked to the ground by Charlie's shots. Two of which got up immediately and began running, the third stayed dead with a shot to the head.

I fired at an exposed leg, which knocked the little girl to the pavement. She turned a hate filled stare at me seconds before her head exploded from a shot from above. The two from the shed came sprinting at Charlie and me, and we both fired several shots to halt the attack.

While I reloaded, Charlie fired single killing shots and I circled wide for the remaining three which were by the van. I couldn't fire towards the van, so I holstered my gun and pulled out my trench 'hawk and my knife. The thirteen inches of steel glistened in the morning as I worked around to the front of the van.

"John! Behind you!" Sarah called a warning just in time. One of the zombies had circled back and was coming at me from the back. I knelt down and swung my axe, smashing the blade into the hissing face. The body flew to the side from the impact, but I didn't have time to admire my handiwork, as a second came running from the other direction. This time, the little shit came in low with his arms outstretched. I waited until he was close enough, then I kicked the little sucker up under the chin, cracking his neck and launching him several feet in the air.

When he landed, his teeth still clacked and clicked, and I speared him in the temple to end his troubles. As I pulled the blade out, the last one came charging around the corner, too fast for me to get with the knife. I readied another kick, hoping I wouldn't be bitten in the process.

I needn't have worried. A long, thin silver line split the air and neatly removed the little child's head from its shoulders. The little girl's long blonde hair flew up as the head sailed away, biting and snarling as it went. It bounced once on the parking lot and Charlie walked up to kill it with his tomahawk.

"Nice work, Duncan. I think I may need one of those," I said in admiration.

"Oh, sure, steal another killer idea. First, you take Charlie's idea for tomahawks, and now you want a sword. What if I want to be the only cool one around?" Duncan laughed at his own joke.

Charlie smiled. "The only way for that to happen is if you're alone."

"Stick it, jerky."

'I'm not the idiot who announced to the world we were here, was I?" Charlie asked, eyeballing Duncan.

Duncan looked down. "Was kinda hoping you hadn't seen that."

I didn't pay attention. I was looking at the brush line and single figure that stood there. She was about ten years old, at least I figured from this distance. She had brown, shoulder-length hair and her face was white. Her eyes were deep-set, and from the way she was standing, it looked like she didn't have eyes at all.

In a flash, I drew my .45, firing from the hip. I had only three shots left, but I let them all go as fast as I could pull the trigger, hoping to get lucky one last time.

My bullets went wide, and then my gun went to slide-lock. I reloaded and brought the gun up to level, but by that time, she had jumped back through the brush.

"Damn. Missed," I said to no one in particular.

Charlie looked over to where I was shooting. "Hell, man, had you scored a hit, I would have put down my gun in homage to the master."

"Bullshit, but thanks anyway," I said.

"Thanks for what? You missed an easy shot," Charlie said.

"What? Listen, you..." Whatever else I had to say was lost as about thirty little zombies came crashing through the brush and literally hurtled across the street and parking lot towards us.

We didn't stop to debate anything else. We bolted for the two buildings. Charlie ran for the Whitebreast Inn, while Duncan and I ran for the Double D. It was standard to split up like this, in the hopes to divide the enemy, or if not, then be able to harass and flank him as needed.

Just as we split, Charlie gave one parting shot to Duncan.

"I blame you for this! I was having a really good morning!" After that, he was inside the Whitebreast Inn.

CHAPTER 48

Duncan and I burst through the front doors of the Double D and immediately started throwing tables and chairs in front of the glass. The only thing we were hoping to do was to slow them down.

As we tossed wooden tables and chairs, Duncan commented on the fixture's material.

"Stuff would burn nicely, with all the alcohol soaked into it," he said.

"Good thought, but we haven't found the back door yet." I replied, turning a table over to the window. Outside, the first of the zombies reached the windows and crashed against it with a meaty smack. A second hit it and I knew it was only going to be a matter of time. There were about fifteen zombies out there, so I knew we probably had divided them up. The big question was whether they had gone to the other building, or had they circled around back, trying to flush us out into hungry mouths.

"Come on, let's get out of here before they break through," I said, running up the stairs.

"Hang on." Duncan removed a lighter from his pack and took up a small candle that was tossed in the corner. It was one of those little globe candles with the netting around it. He lit the candle, then carried it up and placed it on the railing of the elevated platform. The candle sent weird shadows around the room, illuminating the bodies that still hung from the upper balcony.

We made our way around the platform, heading towards the back. We had to move around the bodies, and I was tempted to cut them down, when Duncan suddenly yelled.

"Shit! Something's got me!" He flailed at the back of his neck, and twisted, trying to get away from whatever had hooked him. I pulled out my flashlight and shined it upwards, looking for whatever had snagged Duncan. I thought some wire or some kind of Christmas lights had caught him.

I did not expect one of the hanging ladies to have grabbed his collar as he went by, holding on tightly as her neck stretched and twisted in the rope collar she had on. Her eyes were dead, and her mouth was open, allowing her swollen tongue to extend outward grotesquely. Her blue face twisted and turned, and I was actually surprised her neck was able to support her.

"Oh, boy. Hold on." I swung quickly with my blade and severed the arm, causing Duncan to stumble forward and the zombie to swing back. I stepped up and pulled the hand off of Duncan, who was vastly relieved to be loose.

"Thanks man. What the fuck, dude? Why did these women kill themselves?" he asked.

I shined the light around the room, and sure enough, four more sets of eyes looked back at me, and here and there, a slender arm rose to try and grasp what was too far out of reach.

"I'd guess they had been infected somehow, and figured to die together. Who knows?" I wiped off my blade and kept moving, the sounds of the little zombies slamming into the glass motivating me to move further to the back. Behind us, the lone candle flickered and sputtered.

We reached the back and ducked through the Employees Only door. I kept moving towards the back, around cases and cases of liquor. Duncan's eyes were huge as he surveyed the inventory.

"Man, this would go for a good buck back home," he said. He was right, too. Since the Upheaval, no one really had bothered to try to make alcohol anymore, so the real stuff was rare and highly prized.

I didn't say anything as I found the back door. It was a simple grey affair with a handmade sign that read 'Keep Clear'. I figured it had to be the right one. I pushed the door carefully, just allowing a crack to appear. It wasn't much, but the sun was bright enough that the little crack allowed a great deal of light in. My eyes, after being used to the dark, smarted a little from the brilliance.

Another smack sounded in the darkness, and this time it had a different quality to it. I figured we had a minute before the window broke open completely. I also figured we might as well use what we have here to take out a few more zombies.

"Grab some bottles and a couple of candles!" I said. "Follow me!"

Duncan knew me well enough to know this was not one of those times to argue. He grabbed a couple of spare candles and followed, not really sure what I was up to.

I ran to the furthest table from the back, and placed a candle on the table. Lighting it, I placed the bottle of alcohol directly over the flame. There was enough of a mouth around the candle jar that air could get in, keeping the candle lit. Duncan did the same with another table closer in, and I did another on my side while he did the same on his.

Running back, there was a crack, and then a crash, as the front window caved in. Duncan didn't waste any time, he shot the candle on the railing and we both watched as the jar blew apart, scattering candle bits everywhere, lighting nothing at all.

"Oh well. It's the thought that counts," he said.

"Keep telling yourself that," I said as a small head peeked up over the edge of the platform. I figured what the hell, and lined up a shot. Imagine my surprise when I scored a hit and the head and body flew backwards.

"I think my way's better," I said, running for the back.

"Show off," Duncan pouted.

We reached the Employees Only door and spun around. About a dozen little zombies were swarming over the railing, dropping to the floor and scurrying through the tables. I didn't waste any time and fired a shot at the bottle over the candle on the table closest to me. The bottle exploded and the alcohol caught fire, causing a huge fireball to suddenly bloom in the dark club. I struggled to see, as my night vision was ruined, and Duncan blew the next bottle.

The little zombies stopped in their tracks and we used the precious seconds to blow the other bottles, shaking the railings with the concussions and causing the hanging zombies to twitch and flail. The alcohol flames covered a large area, and the club was well lit for a minute. We used the light to shoot two more, and then we dashed through the door and secured it from the other side. Tiny hands pounded on the door while we made our way out the back. Duncan managed to grab a couple of bottles of booze as we went past, and we were outside quickly.

"Do you think the place will go up?" Duncan asked, securing the alcohol in his backpack. He had two bottles of Bombay Sapphire, something that was expensive, even back when you could go to the store and buy it. He could trade one of those bottles for a house these days.

"Not sure," I said, scanning the area for threats. The place seemed quiet, but I knew that was just a temporary state. "Come on, help me push." I went over to the dumpster and started pushing it towards the front of the building. It was a decent sized one, so I hoped it would do for what I had in mind.

"What's up?" Duncan asked, pushing on the other side.

"I want to use this to try and block the front door, maybe we can take out a lot more of those little things."

"Good call." Duncan redoubled his efforts and we managed to push the dumpster to the front of the Double D in a less than a minute.

When we reached the front, Duncan checked the area and said he thought the little ones were still inside. Smoke was pouring out of the broken door, and I hoped we could finish off a good number of the little beasts.

We pushed the trash dumpster into place, and with a huge effort from both of us, we managed to tip it over with a big crash. A couple more pushes and the big metal container was effectively blocking the broken area. They could still get out, but they would have to get through the glass again, and the way the inside was burning, I would guess they didn't have much time left. I could see the flames creeping higher up the walls, and the areas inside the platform were a mass of fire and smoke. Good enough. The hanging zombies were on fire, and their bodies were lighting the balcony from which they hung. In a little while, the roof was going to be on fire and this was going to be one that could be seen for miles.

As we walked away, a small boy crashed into the glass, his clothes burned away and his hair on fire. He stared hate at us from inside the Double D, and pounded futilely on the thick glass. As we watched, the flames began to lick at his feet and then his legs. He didn't have much time left, and I could see he was clearly frustrated. In all honesty, given what we had been through in the last few days, I couldn't have cared less.

CHAPTER 49

We cautiously went across the parking lot, keeping a careful eye out for any zombies. Duncan kept watch on the brush, but there were no other attacks. The Double D behind us creaked and groaned from the fires raging inside, and I was waiting for the alcohol to explode and wipe out anything left in the bar.

There was nothing outside on the front, and I used the opportunity to get over to the truck and grab a rifle. Duncan grabbed one as well, and I have to admit I was much more comfortable with the additional firepower.

We edged around the side of the building, and standing at the back was a little zombie. His attention was focused away from us, and I figured there was no point in being quiet, so I lined up a shot and popped him in the head. He dropped to the ground and another zombie stuck her head around the corner, but she ducked back before I could get another shot off.

"Well, since those zombies are still here, everyone else should still be alive," I said.

Duncan opened his mouth and before he could speak, the front windows of the Double D blew out, spewing flame and smoke. A small body flew out of the explosion as well, but it landed heavily and didn't get back up. Smoke billowed out up to the sky, joining the clouds already crossing the great blue. We both looked at the burning building for a second, and I could see parts of the roof that were about to succumb to the flames. Once a second opening happened, the building would be an inferno.

We moved further around and a third zombie came into view. Duncan brought up his rifle and killed it quickly, and then we ran over to the back, figuring to end this quickly.

But our fight was short lived, since there was nothing back here. The door was closed, and I didn't think anything had gotten in there. I pulled out my radio and called in.

"Charlie? Sarah? Tommy? Anybody there? Over." I waited for a minute, and then repeated myself.

A second after I finished, the radio came alive. "John? Everything all right?" It was Charlie, and he sounded a little agitated.

"We're good. Probably killed a good twenty zombie kids out here. Had to burn down the Double D to do it."

"Where are you?" Sarah's voice came through next.

"We're outside your building. Where did the zombies go?" I was actually very curious about this. They weren't out here with us, unless they were really well hidden, and it didn't seem like they had gone anywhere else.

"We killed a few, but the rest scattered. Hold on, we're coming out," Charlie said.

That made sense. No point in wasting batteries on a conversation we could have face to face. We waited for a few minutes, and as we waited, I ran over in my mind what we might have learned from our encounters. The kids were fast. They were smarter than the average zombie was, and they somehow had a leader and were able to communicate with each other. They attacked as groups, never as an individual, and they seemed to be following some purpose. If I hadn't seen them up close, I would have thought they were alive, just twisted in a way that was simply evil. Of course, that wouldn't explain how they could make zombies out of adults if they weren't dead themselves, but after the Upheaval, I was taking a lot of this on the fly.

The rest of the crew came out of the Whitebreast and stood at the ready, waiting to see if the rest of the zombies were going to come out and play. When it looked like they were really gone, I turned to Sarah and asked the obvious question.

"So, Mrs. Lincoln, how was the show?"

Sarah shrugged. "Not much of one. We got Charlie inside and we readied for an attack. Nothing really happened."

I stared for a second. "Really? That's it?"

"That's it. Looks like you had all the fun." Sarah gave me a little hug. "I'm glad you made it out okay."

"Me, too. I wonder where they went?" I was finding this extremely strange.

Charlie spoke up. "Why don't we mount up and get the hell out of here, and try to get ahead of them again and set up some kind of ambush? We can whittle away at them and reduce them to running small groups. By the time the army gets here, they can surround and finish them off."

"With the group that near, I can't see why not. Let's get out of here and get chasing. Tommy, did you see anything about where they were headed when you were on the roof?" I asked.

Tommy nodded. "Looks like the same thing we've been chasing all along. They're headed east. What path they're taking, I couldn't tell you for sure, but I do know for sure I am not about to go plunging into that brush without air support."

"I hear you. All right, let's get rolling and see what we can see," I said, moving to the truck. I spent ten minutes refilling every magazine I had, and making sure all of the spare rifles and handguns were loaded and ready as well.

Twenty minutes later, we were racing down Idaho Street, trying to get ahead of the threat we knew was out there. We drove about two miles, and then stopped at an abandoned farm. I gave Duncan the biggest binoculars we had and sent him up the side of the silo. I figured he could spot nearly any movement a hundred feet up in the air.

Duncan easily climbed to the top of the silo. After fifteen minutes, he came down and asked to look at a map. Sarah gave him the roadmap we had been using, and he looked at it for a long minute.

Afterwards, he announced quite calmly, "I haven't got a clue as to where they are."

I cursed. "Dammit, they must have gone south when we went north." I looked at the map to make sure I was where I thought I was. "Dammit." I folded the map and got back in the truck. Sarah tossed up an eyebrow and I answered, "I guessed wrong, they went south not north."

"Damn. Well, let's get moving. Where are we headed?" Sarah asked.

"We'll take 34 until we reach this road through this forest," I said as I looked over the map with her. "With luck, we'll be able to delay them at the forest."

Sarah nodded and looked worried.

"What's wrong?" I asked, pulling out of the farm's driveway and back onto the main road.

"I don't know, John. I just have a bad feeling about this. Something about you and these little zombies scares the heck out of me, Sarah said.

"I said that at the beginning, remember?" I replied. "I didn't want to go on this trip to begin with."

Sarah said nothing, just looked out the window. When she spoke, it was quiet.

"I just want to get home. I don't know why, but I feel like we need to get home."

"We're headed that way, we just need to track these guys so the army can get them surrounded and finish them off." I tried to sound reassuring, but for some reason, I wasn't so confident.

"I know, I know. Maybe just drive a little faster?"

"Can do."

We drove quickly to 137th Trail, which was a winding road that took us through a heavily wooded area. The trees were nearly on top of the road, and the leaves covered the winding path. Several times, we slipped off the road, unable to see where the pavement ended. Charlie radioed several times, telling us he was having a hard time even seeing, since we were kicking up so many leaves. I nearly hit several deer that were moving across the road, and they looked at me quizzically, as if they had never seen anything like me before. Given the fact that they were young, it was highly probable they had never seen humans before.

After a few miles of twisting roads, we emerged from the edge of the woods into a field. According to the map, we had about a mile to go before we hit the next cross street.

"John! John! John!" The handset yelled at me suddenly and I jumped at the noise. Sarah smiled at my discomfort as she took the radio.

"What is it, Duncan?" she asked, patting my leg.

"The town of Lucas is under serious attack! They're screaming for help up there!"

I looked at the map. Lucas was north of us. We had gone in exactly the wrong direction. Son of a bitch.

I sighed. "All right, let's go. Get ready."

I looked out the windows as we raced to the next road. We had to head east, then north to get to Lucas, which was crazy since had we had turned south only a few hundred yards from Lucas back on 34.

Now we were miles away and likely to be too late to do anything. Only one thing went through my mind as I tried to figure out how these guys were moving through the countryside so quickly.

When were we going to do something right?

CHAPTER 50

We fairly flew up Route 65, which was also called Division Street for some reason. The road was clear, save for the occasional vehicle parked on the side of the road. The cars were rusted and useless, and probably had been there for years.

Several homes broke up the landscape, some fairly large, others small, but with enormous yards. Several looked to be the playground of your typical country folk, several battered cars in the yard, an outbuilding that hadn't seen maintenance in years, and scattered toys about an abandoned play set.

I called back on the radio to Duncan to see if he had heard anything else, but he told me he'd heard nothing for a while now. Sarah and I exchanged a look, and we both knew we were probably too late.

Ten minutes later, we pulled into the southern end of the town of Lucas. Crossing the railroad tracks, we slowly pulled into the main street. I had to be careful of where I drove, since there were bodies everywhere. They were under bushes and by trees, blood trails marking how they had dragged themselves to die. Some bodies were strewn about, as if they had been dragged from places of safety and killed. Throats were torn open, torsos were ripped apart, and faces were mangled and ripped.

Blood was everywhere.

Down each street, the scene was the same. The houses were broken into, and in the ones where we could see inside, there was blood and gore all over the place. One body was draped over a threshold, her hands still gripping the doorframe where she tried to save herself. Her legs had great hunks of meat torn off and the bloody chunks were tossed about the yard.

Other bodies lay in the streets, some old, some young. I could see where some of the attackers had met resistance and gone down with a bullet between the eyes.

Sarah rode silently with her hand over her mouth, shaking her head slowly. I knew how she felt. They had no warning, no way of knowing what was headed their way.

Down every street, it was the same. Broken homes and broken bodies. Back towards the center of town, a large group had made a stand, and they were slaughtered to the last. Blood flowed freely over the ground, and congealed in small pools wherever a depression in the ground happened to be. Most of the damage was centered on the face, neck and arms. It was easy to see how they died. The little bastards would attack, one would get a bite in and then others would join. Soon the victim would pass out from blood loss and that was it.

I radioed in. "Did anyone see anyone alive? Anything at all?" I felt responsible for this massacre. If we hadn't gone south, we would have been here at the attack and may have been able to make a difference.

Rebecca radioed back. "No, John. They're all dead."

Damn. They didn't have much of a chance at all. They never knew what was coming and they certainly weren't expecting the kind of zombie that hit them. As I drove past body after slain body, I had to wonder if this was just a taste of things to come. I just wish I knew how they were traveling! If I had that little clue, then we could set up a trap and blow them away. But as it was, we had no idea.

"John?" It was Charlie.

"Yeah?"

"We need to finish them, you know that."

"I know it. I was just avoiding it." I was too. We had to get out and take care of these once and for all. Otherwise, they were going to come back, and that was an extra mess that I didn't feel like cleaning up.

"Whenever you're ready."

"No time like the present."

We pulled over and got out of our vehicles. The air had a coppery smell that came and went in strength, and we could hear flies starting to approach the meat on the ground. From the back of the truck, I pulled out a real pickaxe, one with a wide metal blade offset by a twelve-inch spike. It was ungainly, but the best things for the groundwork we had to do. Charlie grabbed a similar one and both of us set about the grim task of spiking the bodies so they wouldn't come back.

We moved quickly, stepping on the heads and planting the spike into the skull of the deceased. We had done this a number of times before, but you never got fully used to it. Killing a zombie was one thing. Even the most hard-core pacifist had to admit the zombie was trying to kill you and you acted in self-defense. But the systematic skull popping of people who were unmoving, and sometimes looked like they were sleeping, well, that was another matter.

The hardest ones were the kids. It was such a shame that they had managed to survive the upheaval as babies, only to fall prey to an anomaly like the kids we were fighting.

We worked silently, while Duncan and Tommy searched the houses for survivors. Rebecca and Sarah took the vehicles and circled the town, looking for anyone who might have fled the carnage and was out in the countryside, too terrified to return. I had my doubts we were going to find anyone, but we had to try.

I was finishing off a couple that had apparently died together, when Charlie called me over to where he was. He was standing by a small body, and by the looks of it, it had been one of the attackers that had been taken down. A large bullet hole was centered on the forehead, surrounded by blackened flesh. The body was sprawled out on the ground, as if it had been thrown back. Given the size of the hole and the obvious point-blank range at which the gun was fired, this one had met someone tougher that he was.

"What's up?" I didn't understand why Charlie was calling me over there. I had seen these guys before.

"I wanted you to take a look at something, it just seemed odd to me, but a second opinion never hurt," Charlie said.

I shrugged. "Talk to me."

Charlie pointed at the dead zombie's feet. They were bare of shoes, and the soles were pretty torn up. Bits of rock and grass were imbedded in the dead flesh, and there were a couple of small, black balls that were stuck in the flesh.

"What are those?" I asked.

Charlie nodded. "I saw those, too, and was wondering if you had any idea where they might have picked up something like that."

I pulled my knife and pried out one of the black balls. It was heavy, and mostly spherical, although it had a kind of point on one part of it. Taking my lighter out, I burned off the zombie gunk, killing any residual virus that might have been lurking around. After the ball had been burned, I looked closely, and I saw that it was made of iron or steel.

"Huh. Wonder where he picked this little thing up?" I asked.

"Good question," said Charlie. "I'd say wherever he picked it up, there had to have been a lot of them, "

"Why's that?"

"No way could he have picked up two on his travels. One, I would believe, but two? No way." Charlie replied.

I had to admit it made sense. I believe in coincidences as much as the next person, but sometimes you had to take the leap and go from coincidence to pattern.

"All right, we'll keep our eyes peeled for anyplace that might have a lot of these. We'd stand a better chance of following these little bastards if we knew what they were running on." I was actually hopeful. I had a feeling this was a break we were going need, and if we weren't careful, it would be the only break.

"We'd better get back to work. It's been nearly an hour and we don't want to give these guys any chance at getting up," I said, turning back to the zombies at hand.

"Oh, damn." I didn't feel the need for anything more descriptive.

"What? Oh, damn." Apparently, Charlie didn't either.

In front of us, about fifteen zombies slowly began to creak upright. They moved, slowly, painfully almost, unfolding themselves from the ground that had lapped up their spilt blood. All fifteen had locked their eyes on Charlie. We stared as if we had been caught killing their brothers with a pickaxe. Never mind, that it exactly what we were doing. It was still creepy to have a horde of zombies silently accusing us of it.

"Now what?" Charlie asked. "The heavy weapons are on the trucks."

"Hang on," I said, cocking an ear to the wind.

Around the corner, the truck came squealing in, causing the zombies to turn towards the new sound. Sarah swung the vehicle wide, and then slammed on the breaks, skidding the heavy truck sideways and slamming the tail end into a dozen zombies. Most were killed on impact, and the momentum of the truck literally threw the zombies fifteen yards away. Sarah quickly put the truck in reverse, and then knocked aside and killed a dozen zombies. She put it back into drive, and pulled away from the rampage. Two zombies were still standing, so Charlie and I hurried over to finish them off.

"Watch your step," I cautioned. "Some of these aren't fully dead yet, "I said this as a zombie skull snapped at my foot as I planted a spike in its skull.

"No kidding. Hey!" Charlie stumbled as a head grabbed his pant cuff and held on. Charlie choked up on the pick and crushed the offender's skull, pulling his pants free.

Sarah came out of the truck, and used her pistol to kill several zombies on her side.

"That it?" She called.

"That should do it," I said, spiking a final zombie. "Any word on the others?

"Rebecca was helping Tommy and Duncan finish off a small horde on their side," Sarah said.

"Cool. Any survivors?" I hadn't expected any, but I could always hope.

Sarah smiled. "As a matter of fact, yes."

"Really?" I was incredulous. I figured we were going to strike out again.

"Rebecca picked them up. It was a family of four that made it into the woods and managed to stay hidden up in a deer stand."

"I'll be damned. Come on, Charlie, let's take care of business, and then let's go see those survivors."

CHAPTER 51

We finished off the last of the zombies, broken or otherwise, and took a minute to flame off our picks. That done, we climbed aboard the truck and headed north, the results of our handiwork still spread out all over the ground. Nothing we could do for it, we had zombies to chase.

On the north side of town, Duncan and Tommy were washing off the side of the van with a bucket of water and a couple of kitchen mops they had found somewhere. The side of the van was one huge bloodstain, and the water sluicing off of it was a dark red that flowed across the street into the storm drain.

"We've got survivors!" I called out.

Tommy waved and Duncan raised a hand in acknowledgement. They would cruise the town, dealing with any zombies left over, and see if they could get a handle on where the little suckers went. For some reason, I kept thinking about those little steel balls stuck in the feet of the little zombie.

Rebecca was standing with the family as they stood by the tree. They looked haggard and worn out, as I'm sure I would be after hearing my town get killed. I got out and sized up the couple. The man was tall and well built, and his wife was a thin, muscular woman who looked more than capable of taking care of herself. She was hugging her children, and taking turns kissing each one on the top of their heads.

"You must be Talon," the man said, holding out his hand. "Name's Greg. Greg Holder. This is my wife Gina, and these are the twins, Paul and Grace."

"Nice to meet you," I said. "You sure picked a good day to wander the woods."

Greg's face was ashen. "What the hell hit us, Talon? One minute we were just a nice community, and then all of a sudden these little demons are tearing us apart! I saw the way things were going in the first five minutes and knew we didn't have a chance but to run."

"You did exactly the right thing. If you'd have stayed, you all would have been killed," I said. "Do you have any transportation? We need to get moving and I'm sure you'd like to leave this town behind."

Holder looked a bit sheepish. "Actually, we don't. We decided as a community not to have cars so we could use the gas for our farm equipment."

Well, that didn't make things easier. "Okay, we could find you a ride to the nearest town, would that work?" I asked, wanting to get going before we lost more daylight and maybe another town.

Rebecca spoke up, "I said we could take them. That's all right, isn't it, John? Charlie?"

Inwardly I cursed and I saw Charlie lower his eyes. I knew he was thinking the same thing I was, but there it was and we couldn't take it back.

I gave in. "Yeah, we can drop you off. Do you need anything from your house?"

Gina spoke up. "We're not going back into town for anything. Please just get us out of here."

"Done. We'll pick up our comrades and be on our way. Ma'am?" I asked.

"Yes?"

"Do me a favor and make sure your kids don't look out the window when we go back into town. Thanks." I knew it would be a mess and I didn't want to deal with it.

We piled into the truck and radioed for Duncan and Tommy to meet us on the east side. We were going to follow 34, which seemed to be the best thing for chasing these Zs, but for whatever reason we kept missing them.

The Holder family stayed in the van and Sarah and I led the way. I was feeling slightly sick, knowing that my decision to go south had been wrong and we were too late to do anything about Lucas. I hoped the next town would be spared that same fate.

The sun was behind us as we drove, and I tried to make it as fast as I could, but several times, I had to slow to nearly a stop and navigate around a deep crevasse in the road. Sarah seemed to sense my mood and tried to alleviate the hard feelings I had about it.

"No way you could have known, John. These things aren't like anything we've seen. You couldn't predict them, even if you had a month to study them," Sarah said, putting a hand on my leg.

I covered her hand with mine. "I know and I accept it. But it seems weird we just keep missing. It's almost like they already know where we're going to be, so they just work around it until it becomes our turn to fight." I stared out the windshield. "I just wish we could get ahead of them and be sure of their coming. Then we could deal a blow that would finish them off for good."

"We will, John," Sarah said. "Anything else?"

"Well, now that you mention it, I really want to get home to our boys. We've been gone a lot longer than I wanted to and I am getting really anxious to be home," I said.

"We'll get there, John. The army is on its way and we're not too far from the border. Have faith." Sarah smiled sweetly.

Faith. Hadn't thought about that word in a long time. Good for other people, I know my own religious leanings have been severely curtailed in the last few years. Oddly, clergy seemed like some of the first to go when the Upheaval hit. It was weird, but I guess if your congregation is running to your church seeking sanctuary, it makes sense that the odds of one of them being infected were pretty good.

Ten miles outside of Lucas we found the town of Russell. I didn't know what to expect, but we readied ourselves for anything. At this point, I was just trying to get lucky, since smart was eluding me.

Russell, we discovered, had been abandoned a long time ago, and was just a small town becoming smaller as more and more homes and buildings fell over. One side of the town had been literally smashed to pieces, making us wonder if a tornado had tried to take out the town.

Greg and Gina were happy with it, and were grateful for the lift away from their old home. They were used to the abruptness of life after the zombies came, and their kids seemed like they were used to it as well.

As we shook hands goodbye, I offered to do a quick sweep of the town, but Greg said he would do fine. I offered him one of our extra rifles, and he gratefully took one of the .22 bullets we had. If nothing else, I knew he'd be able to put meat on his family's table.

We left Russell and the Holders and headed back to 34. I had been thinking things over and decided the only way we might get a handle on this would be just to run like hell for the river, alert the towns along the way, and listen for trouble as it came to us. We'd be sacrificing some people, but in the end, we didn't have much choice. At least we could warn them.

CHAPTER 52

I went over the plan with the rest of the crew and they seemed to accept the idea, although somewhat reluctantly. I wanted to hear what everyone had to say, so I threw it out there.

Charlie spoke first. "I think you're probably right. We can't do much more than warn people, and if Lucas was any evidence of what these Zs can do, then we're going to need the backup of the army and a good place to make a stand."

Rebecca spoke next. "I just don't know. I feel like we're abandoning these people, and that doesn't feel right, either."

Duncan piped up. "I'm with Charlie. We don't have the resources, and we've been lucky so far. If they had come at us full force back at the silos and the strip clubs, then we wouldn't be here."

Tommy nodded his approval and Sarah did the same. In all honesty, we didn't have much choice. We could run around all over Iowa trying to put out fires and in the meantime, the perpetrators were wandering around making zombies and putting a general strain on a relatively fragile peace.

"So what's the plan then?" Duncan asked.

"Basically, we're running and yelling. We need to get the army on this side of the river, position them so they can report activity, then sweep in and take care of the problem once and for all. We need to broadcast to everyone who can listen to watch their borders and seal up tight, at least for the next couple of weeks. We don't know where these suckers are going to be, so until we do, we need to cast a wide net," I said. "If we catch them, without army support, we'll have to run and gun. We'll get killed otherwise."

We piled into the van and truck and Sarah spread out the map. "Our next big town is Albia, but I'm not sure anyone is there," Sarah said, frowning.

"There ought to be a small community there. We set one up in each of the dead cities just to be relays for messages and communication. If they're still there, we should be able to touch base pretty quickly," I said, turning onto 34 again.

Sarah nodded. "I remember. We put them in place as an outpost, with the thought that strays would come in eventually."

We called anyone that had been chased into the weeds by the zombies strays. That accounted for a lot of people, but most of them had been re-established with communities and places somewhat near their homes. If they were from a big city that had no hope of ever being re-taken, they found other places to live. Some wandered for years. Others would just stay in the weeds, preferring the safety of the open to the confines of civilization.

"Think they're still alive?" Sarah asked.

"They've got pretty powerful radios, so I'd be surprised if they hadn't heard our conversations so far and realized something was up," I said.

It was about twenty miles to Albia, so we were there pretty quickly. We found the station and the twenty people who were manning it. They were barricaded in a brick building that stood a little apart from other structures. They were located south of the city proper, and as we approached, I could see a man on the roof with some big binoculars. I hoped he had seen something and could tell us where they went.

We parked by the building, and greeted the two women who came out. I explained what we were up to and they said they had been hearing a lot of chatter all day and were curious as to what was going on. I explained the situation, and they were very helpful in getting us in touch with several communities.

The overall picture was very weird. We contacted several communities in the area, everyone we thought might be in line with an attack, and none of them had reported anything out of the ordinary. I told them to keep a very sharp eye out and be wary of night attacks. Everyone had a hard time believing me when I said these things were smart, but they understood very clearly, when I described what happened to the town of Lucas.

I then got in touch with Colonel Freeman, who was in charge of the portion of the army that had been sent to assist. I was pleasantly surprised to learn he had crossed the river, and was waiting to hear from me for deployment. Looking at a map, I realized there was a substantial river at Ottumwa, and between

Chilicothe and Eldon, there was only seven places to cross the river.

I asked Colonel Freeman how fast he could get his troops to those positions, and after a brief pause, he told me it was possible to be in position in three hours. I nearly jumped out of my chair. Three hours! We had them! If they were on a straight course, we'd have them caught!

I calmed down and told the colonel that would be fabulous, and sooner would be better if it could be done. He replied that scouts should reach the Ottumwa area within an hour and a half, or two hours, tops.

We left shaking hands with the people of Albia, and reminded them to stay vigilant. We weren't sure where the Zs were, and until we'd wiped them out, they needed to be very careful.

Back at the vehicles, I relayed what I had spoken to the colonel about, and the crew took the news very well. Mostly it consisted of a lot of 'about time' and sentiments like that.

Charlie was the one who brought things to a worry, though. "Nightfall is in three hours. Think everyone will be in place by then?"

I shrugged. "Can't do anything but try. Let's get ourselves there and wait for the cavalry."

Back in the truck, Sarah gave my hand a squeeze, and I smiled at her. I hoped to hell this worked, because I sure didn't feel like chasing this band of zombies across the damn country any more than I already had.

CHAPTER 53

We drove for Ottumwa, and made it there with plenty of time to spare. Ottumwa was a river community, and hadn't been completely spared by the Upheaval. But the citizens had learned how to deal with the zombies early and had made their defenses on the land in the oxbow that wound through the southern portion of town. The northern part had survived, but the southern had not. The citizens of the north didn't want to deal with the constant threat of zombies from the other side of the river, so a three-year campaign of hunt and kill ensued, mostly in the winter months.

It seemed to have worked. We drove in from the west and there was no activity whatsoever. The houses and businesses on the south end were empty, but they weren't falling apart just yet. The road crossed the oxbow, and it was easy to see how well that little bit of land could be defended. Ten determined people with enough ammo could ruin a zombie horde's whole day.

I met with the town leaders, all solid men and women, and told them the whole story. They gave us what supplies we needed, and got the citizenry informed of the coming of two armies; one friendly and the other decidedly not. The people were going to stay homebound until given the all clear, and would not engage any of the enemy unless their lives or the lives of their loved ones were at stake. It was a hard thing to say, but they had to refuse to help their neighbors if they wanted to survive.

An hour after we got to the city, the advance scouts from the army arrived. There were ten men and they were heavily armed. They had been briefed about the situation, and I instructed them to head north to the road crossing at Chilicothe. That was the farthest bridge from us, and I hoped if it was blocked it would be enough to send the zombies further south to look for a place to cross, which would put them right in our crosshairs. If the zombies went north, I had no idea what I was going to do.

An hour and a half later, Duncan reported to me that the army proper was pulling into position on the east side. I left my comfortable spot at a small café and waved Charlie to join me. We took the truck over to the rendezvous point and found Colonel Freeman.

It was an awesome sight to see a thousand men assembled for battle. There were heavy weapons mounted on a variety of vehicles, but the majority was Hummers. Big trucks carrying supplies were pulling up as we got out of our pickup, and a nervous-looking corporal brought us over to a small RV that served at the Colonel's command post.

The corporal stuck his head in the door. "Sir! John Talon to see you, sir!"

"Of course! Send them in!" Came the reply. Charlie and I stepped into the vehicle, and I was impressed with the sparse furnishings. This was a working command center, not a place for a commander full of himself. Colonel Freeman met us in the center area, shaking hands and smiling broadly.

"John Talon. By God, I've wanted to meet you. Heard so much about you! I almost started to think you were just a legend!" Freeman had an easy way about him, and I was glad he wasn't someone who seemed to be only interested in furthering his career. He was about five foot five, and seemed to be made of pure energy. The man practically vibrated, and even in the confined space of the RV, he managed to find room to pace and move around.

"Nice to meet you too, Colonel. This is Charlie James. He's been with me through nearly everything," I said.

"Dear God! Charlie James! I am in the presence of greatness. The two heroes of the Zombie Wars! Here! In my office! My wife will never believe this. Well, enough gushing, how can we fix this little problem?"

I outlined the situation, letting the little colonel know we had a unique situation here thanks to the geography of the region to finally trap and finish off the zombies that have been creating havoc throughout the state of Iowa.

Colonel Freeman listened intently, and then asked. "How do you want to handle the area here?"

I shook my head. "I gave you the details, Colonel. You're in charge of your army, not me. You know them best and know the best places to put your people. I never stand in the way of experts."

Colonel Freeman stood and shook my hand. "Heard that about you, too, Mr. Talon. Good. We'll fix these little bastards and do it right." He shook our hands and we left. As we were leaving, Colonel Freeman was yelling for his orderlies and his officers. I felt we were in pretty good hands.

As we returned to the truck, Charlie spoke for the first time. "Got a good feeling about him. Maybe this mess will end here."

I looked at the darkening sky. "I hope so."

We drove back to our wives and settled in for the night. We weren't going to be part of the fight, so we had very little to do. The river was very beautiful in the evening, and Sarah and I spent a good deal of time out on the porch of our hotel room just watching and listening to the river as it flowed by.

Sarah was standing in my arms as I leaned on the railing. Her hair was right below my face and it only took a small movement to breathe her in. She leaned back against me and put her hands on my biceps.

"I miss my babies," she said. "I hope everything's okay."

"They'll be fine. We should be home tomorrow if everything goes the way it's supposed to," I said.

"Do you think this Colonel is up to the job?"

"His men seem to trust him, and that's a big endorsement of his abilities. I think they can. They know what they're fighting, so they won't hesitate. And they are mobile, so when the attack comes, they can shift positions quickly and reinforce or chase as needed."

Sarah pulled my arms off the railing and wrapped herself in them. I used the opportunity to kiss her head. She raised her face to mine and after a while, we forgot completely the danger headed our way.

CHAPTER 54

I woke up feeling remarkably refreshed. Sarah was already awake, and dressed, having let me sleep a little longer than I normally did. I stretched out my arms, and then dropped to do some push-ups and sit-ups. It was a routine I had gotten away from in recent months, and I was now trying to bring it back. My shoulders told me I needed a lot of work.

After getting dressed, Sarah and I went back to the truck and pulled out some supplies for breakfast. Duncan and Tommy were already there, and I could see Charlie and Rebecca coming down the street from their room.

"Did anything happen last night?" I asked, breaking off a chunk of my homemade granola bar.

Tommy shook his head. "All quiet, from what I understand. See for yourself. It's almost strange." He pointed to the river and I climbed up on the truck bed and took a look.

From my vantage point, I could see five of the river crossings and on the center of each one, there was a platoon of soldiers. They had piled up sandbags and were sitting patiently behind their barricades, quietly drinking coffee and likely thinking their officers were nuts.

"So nothing happened? Did we miss them?" I asked as I jumped off the truck.

Duncan shrugged. "I don't see how. They were definitely headed this way, and I don't think they went up north. You don't suppose they just stopped somewhere, do you?"

I hadn't an answer for that one. Everything we'd seen so far indicated they weren't inclined to stop anywhere.

Colonel Freeman came speeding up to us in a pickup, and fairly hopped out before the vehicle had come to a stop.

"Morning all! Quiet night, hey? Maybe we'll see some activity today. Sure would be nice to fight in daylight. Zombie killing in the dark is creepy. No reports of activity from anyone last night, letting the men sleep a little this morning." Freeman got out all of this without taking a breath.

"No answer for you, Colonel. Hate to see you wasted a quick march on a wild goose chase," I said seriously.

"No trouble, Mr. Talon! The men need practicing things like that, cause you never know when it might be useful. Rapid deployment! That's what killed the Romans. Couldn't move fast enough. Not like this army!" Colonel Freeman was very sure of himself and his men, and I could see why they liked him. It was hard not to like a perpetual optimist.

"Sir!" The corporal driving the truck stuck his head out the window.

"What is it, Corporal?"

"Sir, the command post reports the town of Batavia is under attack!"

"Damn! Where is Batavia?" Colonel Freeman turned to the driver.

"Don't know sir. Report says they got hit early this morning."

Colonel Freeman turned to us. "Got a map?"

Duncan reached into the van and pulled out a thick folder. He rummaged a bit, and then handed a highway map of Iowa to the Colonel. Freeman opened the map, found our location, and then began checking the area to the west of Ottumwa.

"Damn, damn, damn. Where the hell is Batavia?" Colonel Freeman was having difficulty finding the town. Obviously, it was important, since it would give us a good line of attack.

Duncan looked over the diminutive soldier and scanned the map. "Aw, shit," he said.

I looked at Duncan. "You gotta be kidding me."

Duncan shook his head. "Wish I was. It's..." Duncan looked at the map scale. "About fifteen miles due east on 34."

"Son of a bitch!" I yelled. "How? Somebody tell me how the hell they crossed the damn river in the middle of the night, right under the noses of a thousand men, and managed to stage an attack on a town fifteen miles away?"

Colonel Freeman winced, and I knew he felt responsible. The question was what were we going to do about it?

"Mount up, we gotta move. Colonel, follow if you can. Get to the Mississippi, and if you have to string your men out one per fifty yards, then do it. They will not get past us!" I jumped into the truck and quickly pulled away, the sound of Colonel Freeman shouting at his troops fading in the distance.

Sarah spoke up. "John, how was that possible?"

"I wish to hell I knew, babe. They've managed to get around us at every turn, and I have no idea how. They aren't that smart, and there aren't that many roads. So how are they doing it? What am I overlooking?" I was frustrated to the point of anger, and I was half hoping there was going to be some action at Batavia, because I needed to kill something.

CHAPTER 55

We sped along Route 34, dodging the worst of the potholes and tree branches. It took us a half hour, and we stopped on an overpass to look the situation over.

Batavia was a small town, and by all accounts, it looked like it should have been fairly left alone from the troubles. But this time the trouble came looking for it. I could see several pockets of zombies attacking a few homes, and a larger pocket attacking what looked like a town hall or something.

"Well, here we go again," I said, putting the truck in gear and heading down the ramp. I drove quickly over the streets and headed right for one of the homes. I could see Charlie break away and head towards another.

I slowed down at the last moment and proceeded to plow over several zombies. They went under the tires with an oddly satisfying crunch. I drove around the house, mowing down the zombies I found, and driving over the ones that tried to get up after being hit. Sarah had her gun out and was ready to take on any that tried to hold on to the truck.

After about five minutes, I didn't see any left, so I pulled away from the house and got out of the truck. Three zombies were out of the way when I hit the horde, and they immediately broke off their attack on the house to head in my direction. I stood there for a moment, and Sarah easily shot all three with her Ruger.

"Thanks, honey," I said, moving towards the house.

"Anytime, babe, anytime." Sarah put her gun away and followed.

"Anyone still alive?" I yelled, hoping for an answer.

"In here! Did you get them?" An anxious voice came from behind the door.

"We got them. You coming out or would you like to just stay there?" I had to ask. Some people were funny about strangers.

"Uh. We'll stay here for a while. Did you get them all?"

"Pretty much. We'll be gone in a bit, after that you're on your own."

"Okay! Thanks!"

I shrugged and Sarah did the same. We went back to the truck and carefully got back inside. We would seriously need to clean it off when we had the chance. I drove over to where Charlie had broken off to see if they needed any help. Charlie had done the same thing I had, but there were more zombies on this side. Duncan was outside, slicing up Zs with abandon, while Charlie, Tommy, and Rebecca were a little more precise.

Charlie was stalking a zombie that had wandered off, an old man in faded pajamas. I wondered why he wasn't trying to fight when I realized he was probably deaf. That threw a weird thought into my head. What did a zombie with Alzheimer's do?

Tommy was taking on two of them, knocking one in the knees and bringing it down while he slammed the other in the head, killing it. The dead one fell on top of the animated one, and that one couldn't get up, making it an easy target for Tommy. Rebecca was just finishing killing a teenage zombie, and squaring off with another.

There weren't any left, so Sarah and I just watched for a bit. After another five minutes, they were finished, and came over to the truck.

"How'd you guys do?" Charlie asked, wiping off his 'hawk.

"Used the truck, and Sarah shot three."

"How many did you save?" Duncan asked.

I chuckled. "No idea. They wouldn't come out."

"Weirdoes. Let's see who we saved!" Duncan wandered over to the house and knocked on the door. "Hello? Anybody in there?"

"Is it safe?" came a plaintive voice.

"God, I hope so. Who's in there?" Duncan looked back at us and we had nothing to offer.

"We've got about fifty people in here. Hold on, I have to get the boards away from the door." We heard the sound of a screwdriver working screws out of the boards, and in a few minutes, we were looking at a lot of people streaming out of the house.   They looked around at their fellow townspeople and several went over to possible relatives and knelt beside them.

The man who Duncan had been communicating with stepped out and shook our hands, but we couldn't stay for pleasantries. There was another group of zombies we had to deal with, and that group was larger than these two combined.

CHAPTER 56

We moved to the center of town and saw about thirty zombies attacking what looked like the town hall. It was a building that was roughly square, but built low to the ground, so there were a lot of easily accessible windows. The trouble was the windows were such that you could only open then half way, and the people inside couldn't effectively kill the zombies that were clamoring around the place. They had the tools to do it, from what I could see, but they didn't have the room to swing. They did the next best thing, which was just to push the zombies away from getting into the windows. Trouble was, every time they pushed one away, another took its place.

We parked the vehicles and got out carefully. Several zombies noticed us, so it was just a matter of time before we were under attack. We couldn't use our rifles, since the bullets had a really good chance of hitting a window and killing someone on the inside, which would kind of defeat the purpose.

"All right. Here they come. You want to take them on as a group or split up?" I asked, taking out my pickaxe. For this kind of crowd, I wanted one-shot stops and the pick always delivered.

Charlie looked the crowd over. "Let's just charge them, and when we've hit the end of the first wave, regroup and do it again."

"Last one to the zombies is a mangy stray!" I called out as we all ran towards the oncoming zombies. There was about ten of them that had split from the main group, and they were strung out in a ragged line as they advanced.

We ran right at them and Charlie was first in kills. He cut down a middle-aged woman who was lurching on a broken ankle, and Duncan was next with a kill on a tall zombie. He looked really cool doing it, as he jumped up and used his sword to hack the zombie's head in half.

I walked right up to a man whose arms were covered in bites and tears, and smashed his head in without breaking stride. Sarah tripped up her zombie before killing it, and Rebecca finessed a knife stab right between the eyes of the one that confronted her.

Tommy had two come at him, and he slipped right between them both. When they turned and bumped into each other, they were confused enough to give him a second to shove his knife into the back of the head of one, then he kicked the other over and spiked its head as well.

Charlie killed another two, and I added one to my score as well. Duncan cut the legs off on another, and managed to lop its head off as it fell.

"I think Duncan wins for coolest kill," Tommy said.

"I'd have to agree, that was pretty awesome," I said.

"Here they come again," Charlie said. "And yeah, that was well done."

Duncan just smiled as Sarah and Rebecca rolled their eyes.

We killed the next group, and the next, and then spent the next few minutes going around and killing the zombies that were preoccupied with fighting the people inside the building. There was a moment when a person inside the building accidentally poked Tommy, but other than that, we had no injuries.

Once the people inside realized the danger was over, they came outside and looked over the carnage. There were a lot of sad moments, especially when people went over to their relatives and friends.

I found a man standing apart and approached him to see if he had any answers.

"Hey. You okay?" I asked.

"Yeah, thanks. Thanks for your help. We kind of had a standoff there."

"What happened? Do you know?" I wanted to make sure I was chasing the same ghosts I had been chasing for the last four days.

The man shook his head. "Not really sure. We'd gone to bed like we'd done for a while, and then suddenly there was a general alarm that we had zombies coming up from the south. Standard procedure was to retreat to the hall and we'd talk care of it from there." He looked around. "Sure didn't see this coming."

"What time did they hit you?" I was curious to see how far ahead of us they were.

"Can't say, maybe around two or three in the morning." The man clearly wasn't sure, but it did tell me that our little group had gotten ahead of us again and we were chasing their tails.

"All right, we'll get out of your way. You have a lot to do." I signaled to my crew and we met back at the rear of the pickup.

"They got hit early this morning, which makes sense if they got past us around midnight. If I was paranoid, I'd say these attacks were just meant to slow us down, but that's giving a lot of credit to the zombies," I said.

"Maybe that's the problem," Sarah said.

"What is?" Asked Rebecca, who was cleansing her weapon.

"Maybe we're not giving them enough credit. If we treated them like they were fully functioning humans, then we'd stop being surprised at what they do and get down to stopping them." Sarah replied.

I had to admit it made sense. "Well, then we need to figure out how they are traveling. Where's that map?" I rummaged around, pulled out the map, and gave it to Tommy. "Here's your job. Look at the map, check every spot we've had contact with the zombies, and then tell me what the connection is. What do they have in common?"

"Gee, that's all?" Tommy asked, but he looked at the map with interest.

"What's our next move?" Charlie asked.

"We won't know for sure until they strike again, but we'll head east, keeping an eye on getting home. The army shouldn't be too far behind."

Duncan piped up. "Actually, I just heard their chatter on the radio and they're ahead of us. Colonel Freeman decided to keep moving and set up a block on the Mississippi. Nothing will get past him there, he swears it."

I tried to believe him, but I knew unless we pinned down how they were traveling, we' lose them again and again. My mind spun over the possibilities, and for some reason I thought back to the little iron balls we dug out of the feet of that little zombie. I had a hunch they were important, but I sure couldn't figure out how.

CHAPTER 57

We left Batavia behind and sped down 34. Thirty miles later, we were on the south end of New London. Duncan reported a small outbreak there, but they had contained it pretty quickly, only losing one person. Apparently, that person had taken a walk by themselves and our friends set upon them. It had happened within the last hour, so we were catching up.

Fifteen miles brought us to the outskirts of Burlington, where we caught up with Colonel Freeman. He had placed his men all along the river, each one heavily armed and ready to go. They were about twenty yards apart, and covered a good distance. The trucks and vehicles had been used to block the road that crossed the Mississippi, and another group of men was sent north to cover the crossing at Muscatine. A third group was sent to Fort Madison to cover the crossing to the south, so there was no place for the zombies to go. Unless they got here ahead of Freeman, I didn't see how we could miss them.

We parked our vehicles on the 34 bridge and stood with Colonel Freeman. We couldn't do anything except wait, but I figured we would be seeing something soon. The little bastards had to be very close. I felt like they were very close. I kept my rifle close, and then assured that all my magazines were full and within easy reach. Everyone else was armed as well, and we fidgeted with little to do. The only one of us that was occupied was Tommy, who was staring intently at the map, trying to find a connection.

Suddenly he shouted. "Railroad!"

"What?" We all kind of jumped, and I was the only one who spoke.

"The railway! That's how they're traveling! Look!" Tommy brought the map over and showed us the connections he had made. "All I did was draw straight lines between the attacks and looked for a connection. I knew the roads were out since we had already covered those, so I looked for something that connected them in another way. That's how they got past us at

Ottumwa. No one had covered the railroad bridge. All of the towns that were attacked had a railway connection."

"Well done, sir, well done." Colonel Freeman was congratulating Tommy along with the rest of the crew. I started to, but something caught my eye. I walked over to the side of the bridge and stared intently to the south.

Sarah and Charlie came over and Sarah put a hand on mine. "Tommy figured it out, John. Now we know how they're moving. John, are you listening?"

I continued to stare, and pointed to the south.

Charlie looked, and cursed.

"What is it?" Sarah asked.

"It's a railroad bridge across the river." As I looked, several small forms raced across the bridge, disappearing into the trees on the other side.

"Oh my God."

"Yeah. They've crossed. They're in Illinois."

THE END

www.severedpress.com

ICE STATION ZOMBIE
JE GURLEY

For most of the long, cold winter, Antarctica is a frozen
wasteland. Now, the ice is melting and the zombies are thawing.
Arctic explorers Val Marino and Elliot Anson race against time
and death to reach Australia, but the Demise has preceded them
and zombies stalk the streets of Adelaide and Coober Pedy.

www.severedpress.com

The Coalition

When the dead rose to destroy the living, Ron Cutter learned to survive. While so many others died, he thrived. His life is a constant battle against the living dead. As he casts his own bullets and packs his shotgun shells, his humanity slowly melts away.

Then he encounters a lost boy and a woman searching for a place of refuge. Can they help him recover the emotions he set aside to live? And if he does recover them, will those feelings be an asset in his struggles, or a danger to him?

THE STATE OF EXTINCTION: the first installment in the **COALITON OF THE LIVING** trilogy of Mankind's battle against the plague of the Living Dead. As recounted by author **Robert Mathis Kurtz.**

www.severedpress.com

RANCID

Nothing ever happens in the middle of nowhere or in Virginia for that matter. This is why Noel and her friends found themselves on cloud nine when one of their favorite hardcore bands happened to be playing a show in their small hometown. Between the meteor shower and the short trip to the cemetery outside of town after the show, this crazy group of friends instantly plummet from those clouds into a frenzied nightmare of putrefied horror.

Is this sudden nightmare related to the showering meteors or does this small town hold even darker secrets than the rotting corpses that are surfacing?

"Zombies in small town America, a corporate conspiracy, fast paced action and a satisfying body count- what's not to like? Just don't get too attached to any character; they may die or turn zombie soon enough!" - Mainak Dhar, bestselling author of Alice in Deadland and Zombiestan

www.severedpress.com

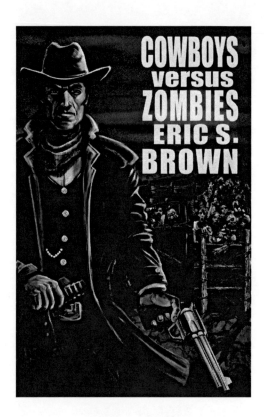

COWBOYS VS ZOMBIES

Dilouie is a killer. He's always made his way in life by the speed of his gun hand and the coldness of his remorseless heart. Life never meant much to him until the world fell apart and they awoke. Overnight, the dead stopped being dead. Hungry corpses rose from blood splattered streets and graves. Their numbers were unimaginable and their need for the flesh of the living insatiable.

The United States is no more. Washed away in a tide of gnashing teeth and rotting, clawing hands. Dilouie no longer kills for money and pleasure but to simply keep breathing and to see the sunrise of the next dawn. . . And he is beginning to wonder if even men like him can survive in a world that now belongs to the dead?

TIMOTHY
MARK TUFO

Timothy was not a good man in life and being
undead did little to improve his disposition.
Find out what a man trapped in his own mind
will do to survive when he wakes up to find
himself a zombie controlled by a self-aware
virus.

JUDGMENT DAY
JE GURLEY

Dr. Jebediah Stone had never believed in zombies until he had to shoot one. A very few Alpha zombies rule smaller hunting packs with the surviving humans as prey. Now, they're mutating into a new species, mortuus venator – dead hunters, capable of reproducing. Jeb Stone searches for his missing wife, taken by the military because she is immune. She and other captured munies supply the blue juice, a temporary vaccine, from their blood. It is a new, dangerous world he finds himself, filled with zoms, the military and their Judgment Day Protocol, merciless Hunters who capture munies for a shot of blue juice, street gangs and famine. Has the world turned on mankind? Is Mortuus Venator the new ruler of earth?

www.severedpress.com

ZOMBIE YOUTH, PLAYGROUND POLITICS

What will the survivors do when everyone over the age of twenty suddenly dies in a viral outbreak? Worse yet, what will they do when the dead refuse stay dead?

A group of students is left trapped in their school as the adults they once relied upon suffer strange symptoms and die, only to return and feed. With no guidance or supervision the students are left to recreate society as they see fit. But not everyone shares their vision of the future...

Zombie Youth: Playground Politics is the first novel in a new series following a group of survivors struggling to stay alive in a world where there are things far worse than zombies.

www.severedpress.com

WHEN THERE'S NO MORE ROOM IN HELL
LUKE DUFFY

Mankind is on the brink of extinction. A deadly plague sweeps the globe like a tsunami causing the dead to rise and prey on the living. When there's no more room in Hell is a horror/action story set in a post-apocalyptic world filled with suspense, drama, humour, grief and action.

While one brother fights his way home through the horrors and confusion of a savage landscape from the 'Meat Grinder' that is Iraq, the other finds himself as the leader of a rag-tag band of survivors striving to survive against the onslaught of the dead.

www.severedpress.com